"It doesn't do any good to fight it."

Sin Buchanan reached around her to take the wineglass from her unresisting fingers. "You can't roll all your emotions and feelings, passions and desires into a neat little bundle and throw them away," he said softly.

Mara tried to ward off her awareness of how close he was. Then his head bent toward her, his jaw and chin brushing her ear. Her heart tripped wildly against her ribs.

"Don't be afraid," he told her. "It's natural for you to respond to your feelings."

The kiss that followed was leisurely, slow, but it opened up a new world for Mara. When he bent to kiss her again, she submitted, surrendered, returned his fire. Either she was learning—or she was becoming a fool!

JANET DAILEY AMERICANA

Janet Dailey
Americana

THE THAWING OF MARA

Harlequin Books

TORONTO • NEW YORK • LONDON
AMSTERDAM • PARIS • SYDNEY • HAMBURG
STOCKHOLM • ATHENS • TOKYO • MILAN

The state flower depicted on the cover of this book is
Mountain laurel.

Janet Dailey Americana edition published December 1987
ISBN 373-89838-X

Harlequin Presents edition published April 1980
Second printing February 1982

Original hardcover edition published in 1980
by Mills & Boon Limited

CHAPTER ONE

"Mara?"

Over the whine of the electric mixer, Mara heard her name called, but she didn't bother to acknowledge it. Instead she added more sugar to the egg whites and continued to beat them until they formed stiff peaks. She was spooning the meringue onto the pie filling when she heard the hum of the wheelchair approaching the kitchen.

"Mara, the mailman just drove by." The chair rolled to a stop inside the room. "I'm expecting some correspondence from Fitzgerald. Will you see if it's come?"

Mara didn't turn around. "I'm busy at the moment, Adam." She continued to spread the meringue thickly over the pie, ignoring the instant of tense silence.

"Will you please stop calling me that?" The request sliced tersely through the air. "I am your father and you will address me as such."

Over her shoulder, Mara glanced at the man whose surname of Prentiss she had rightfully carried since birth. Her heart turned to stone at the sight of the handsome man imprisoned in the wheelchair.

His hair was as black as her own, except at the temple where wisps of silver gave him a distinguished air. They shared the same deep color of eyes. There was enough similarity in their sculpted features that there was no mistaking they were father and daughter.

"I'm not denying my parentage, Adam." Her voice was as cool as her attitude.

He whitened at her continued usage of his given name, his fingers tightening on the armrest of his chair. Mara noted his reaction with indifferent satisfaction and let her attention return to the pie. After swirling the white top into decorative peaks, she opened the door to the preheated oven and set the pie inside to brown the meringue. All the while the man in the wheelchair remained silent.

"It looks good." Her father forced the words out, striving for lightness and a degree of familiarity. "What kind is it? Chocolate, I hope."

"It's lemon," Mara retorted, not changing the temperature of her voice.

"You should make some chocolate cream pie sometime," he suggested.

"I loathe chocolate pie." She set the beaters and bowl in the sink and ran the water from the tap.

"You didn't always hate it." It was almost a challenge. Then his voice became warm and reminiscent. "When you were growing up, we used to argue over who got the last slice of chocolate pie. We usually ended up splitting it."

"That was a long time ago." Her curtness dismissed the idea that the past had anything to do with today.

"Your mother made the best chocolate cream pies

I've ever tasted." Adam Prentiss went on. "I don't know where Rosemary got the recipe, but—"

Mara pivoted. Anger blazed in her dark eyes, burning off the frigid aloofness that usually encased her. It consumed her with an all-enraging hatred.

"How dare you speak my mother's name!" she accused in a seething breath.

"She was my wife," he stated, levelly meeting her glare.

"Was she?" The taunting challenge was drawn through tightly clenched teeth as years of bitterness trembled through Mara. "You conveniently forgot about that when you ran off with that little tramp, didn't you?"

"I didn't forget it," Adam Prentiss denied.

"You had a wife and child." Her voice was rising in volume. You abandoned us without so much as a backward glance!"

"You were only fifteen at the time, Mara," he attempted to reason. "You couldn't know—"

"I was there!" she flared. "I know what happened. When you walked out on my mother for another woman, it killed her. It just took a few years before she literally died. She adored you, she worshipped you. She ate, breathed and slept for you. You were the only thing that mattered to her."

"Do you think I wasn't sorry?" her father retaliated. "Do you honestly believe I didn't wish there was another way? Do you think I didn't care?"

"All you cared about was that young blonde," Mara retorted, and turned away in disgust. "My God, she was only a few years older than I was!"

"I was in love with Jocelyn and I won't apologize for that," he said quietly. "But as strange as it sounds, it is possible to care about two women at the same time. I did care about your mother."

"I don't believe you. I saw the callous way you treated her," she reminded him. "Even before that blonde, you flirted with everything in skirts."

"For God's sake, Mara, those incidents were perfectly harmless." His impatient reply was angry.

"Harmless?" A bitterly amused sound came from her throat. "Yes, mother always used to laugh them off, but I could see the hurt in her eyes. You must have seen it, too. But it never bothered you, did it?"

"I don't have to justify my behavior to you. I've never pretended to be perfect." He was coldly indignant.

"But you managed to convince mother you were," Mara continued her attack with vindictive zeal. "She used to think she was the luckiest woman on earth because she was your wife."

"I was in love with someone else. Do you honestly believe I should have stayed married to your mother when I knew that?" her father challenged. "Both of us would have been miserable if I'd done that."

"So you walked out on her. That way she was the only one who was miserable," she pointed out spitefully.

"All right, I hurt your mother. I admit that," he declared in agitation. "But give me credit for providing for her financially. I turned everything over to her—the house, the land, money, everything I owned except my clothes. I had nothing. I still have nothing. You got it all when she died."

"Did you think she'd leave it to you?" Mara jeered.

"No." It was a sighing answer, a mixture of defeat and exasperation. "Haven't I paid enough, Mara? Jocelyn was killed in the crash that did this to me. I'm permanently crippled. The doctors have even warned that as I grow older, my condition may deteriorate to the point where I won't even be able to get around in a wheelchair."

As the fight went out of his voice, Mara's fiery anger left, too. An icy calm stole through her, cooling her features into a frozen mask and freezing her senses to his plight. She walked to the oven where the curling peaks of the pie's meringue were the color of golden toast.

"If you're attempting to arouse my pity—" with a pot holder, Mara took the pie from the oven and set it on a wire rack to cool "—you're wasting your time."

"I'm attempting to understand you," her father replied wearily. "Why am I here? After my accident you went to the doctors and told them that you were bringing me here and you would take care of me. At the time I thought you'd finally forgiven me. But you haven't. So why am I here?"

"Unlike you, I felt a sense of family obligation." Mara returned the pot holder to its drawer. "Regardless of how I feel about you, you are my father. It's my duty to take care of you."

"And that's why I'm here. Because you consider

it's your duty.'' He studied her, brown eyes measuring brown eyes. "Are you sure I'm not a convenient excuse to shut yourself off from the rest of the world?''

A smile twisted her mouth. "It's my responsibility to take care of you. But I'm sure you don't understand that since you don't know the meaning of the word.''

"You're so righteous, Mara, that I sometimes expect to see a halo circling your head,'' Adam Prentiss commented dryly. "Yet you have few friends. Whenever people invite you somewhere, you always turn them down because you have to stay here to take care of me. Hardly anyone calls anymore.''

"It doesn't bother me.'' Mara lifted her shoulders in an uncaring shrug.

"You rarely went out when your mother was alive, either, did you? You spent most of your time with her.'' There was a shrewd gleam in his look.

"Mother was very lonely after you deserted her.'' The flatness of her statement was calculated to lash at him. "She needed me.''

"You used her as an excuse the same way that you're using me,'' her father accused in a low, quiet voice. "You like to look down on the rest of us from your lofty position of piety. What are you afraid of, Mara? Are you afraid that if you step down from your pedestal, you'll discover you're as imperfect as the rest of us?''

"Believe whatever you wish, Adam. I couldn't care less what you think.'' With a mildly arrogant smile, she turned from him and walked to the coat rack. Taking her wool plaid jacket from an iron hook, she put it on. "I'll go and see if the mailman left anything in our box."

"Go ahead and run from the conversation, Mara," he interposed. "It's as ineffective as shutting yourself away."

At first she made no response as she paused at the back door. When she turned, her gaze sought the man in the wheelchair.

"You're only trying to rationalize your own feelings of guilt, Adam," she said. "You know you need someone to take care of you, but you prefer to pretend that I'm doing it for some other reason because it makes you feel better."

"Oh, Mara!" He shook his head sadly.

Her gaze strayed from him to wander over the old, cozy kitchen. The oak cupboards and cabinets had been installed over a century ago, but time hadn't dulled the rich luster of the wood. The walls were papered in a cheerful yellow and white check design to match the tieback curtains at the windows.

An aging oak table and spindle-backed chairs stood in the middle of the room. The tabletop was covered with a bright yellow cloth, a small wicker basket of red apples and oranges at its center. The floor was covered with a continuous length of white linoleum, speckled with red, yellow and green.

"I know it bothers you that this is my home," Mara said. "You're only here at my sufferance. Knowing how you abandoned us, it probably irritates you to be so dependent upon me. But you're really very lucky, Adam. Here you have a comfortable place to live and you can continue your work. Plus, you not only have me as nurse and housekeeper, but also as a typist and researcher. Why don't you think about that instead of seeking an ulterior motive for something that I'm only doing out of a sense of family duty?''

When she was answered with silence, Mara turned and opened the back door. "Don't let the wind blow your halo off," came her father's biting words of caution.

Her lips thinned as she pushed open the second door, its screen replaced with storm-glass panes. She closed the inner door while stepping outside. The second door swung shut on its own when she released it.

A brick path circled the house to the front entrance, then continued out to the gravel road. There was an autumn chill in the air, September's breath. A few leaves were scattered around on the green lawn even though there hadn't been a killing frost yet. The trees were still full and green, but soon they would be painted with autumn colors. Then the Pennsylvania countryside around Gettysburg would be arrayed in hues of gold and scarlet and rust.

With her hands in her pockets, Mara held her jacket front together and followed the brick walk out to the road. The carriage of her head was naturally high, but after her father's biting rejoinder she held her head even higher. She despised him. The force of the emotion clenched her hands into fists in the pockets of her jacket.

How typical of him to try to make someone else feel guilty! Mara remembered how her mother had anguished over what she had done wrong when he'd run off with that other woman. Mara had insisted it wasn't her fault. The only blame she placed on her mother was for being such a fool over him.

A squirrel scurried around, busily stashing his winter supply of food. Overhead there was a flash of scarlet as a cardinal flitted among the tree branches. But the wildlife didn't draw even a passing interest from Mara.

At the mailbox, she pulled down the door and removed the letters inside. Pausing, she glanced through them. Most were addressed to her father, although there were a couple of bills for her. Typically she received no personal correspondence.

It was true that she had few friends, but she had never felt any great sense of loss at her lack of companionship. In fact, Mara often felt sorry for those who had to constantly be with others. She was content to be alone, not depending on someone else to entertain her. She viewed it as a trait of strength.

Mara's independence was something that had developed over her twenty-two years. Part of it came from her environment, being raised in the country with none of the close neighbors having children her age, and with no brothers or sisters. Part came from the circumstances of her life. Her schoolmates had sympathized with her at her father's sudden departure, but they hadn't understood the sense of betrayal Mara felt.

His desertion of her and her mother for another, younger woman wasn't something that could be kept quiet. Adam Prentiss was a noted Civil War historian, an authority on the Battle of Gettysburg. Everyone in the area knew what had happened and why.

Mara had been in her first month of college when her mother took sick. She had left college and cared for her mother until she died six weeks later. Then there had been the arrangements for the funeral and all the legal business of settling the estate. Finally there had been her father's accident two years ago. All of it had contributed to Mara's unconscious decision to rely on no one but herself.

She closed the mailbox and turned to retrace her steps to the two-story red brick farmhouse with its white windows and door. A car came down the country road. It slowed as it approached and honked its horn. She recognized Harve Bennett, the dark-haired driver.

"I have some good news for you!" he shouted out of the opened car window, and turned into the driveway that ran parallel with the brick walk.

Mara lifted an eyebrow in fleeting curiosity before she started toward the house. His message obviously had something to do with the cottage on the far corner of the property. Harve Bennett was a young real estate man with whom Mara had become acquainted while ironing out some title questions during the settling of her mother's property and estate.

The cottage had once provided rental income. After her father had left, it had become neglected and too run-down to be rented. A few months ago, Harve had finally succeeded in persuading Mara to make the necessary repairs and fix it up. Mara had agreed, partly because her father had advised against it, insisting that she wouldn't be able to recoup the cost through the nominal rent she could charge for the small one-bedroom cottage.

All the major work had been completed a week ago, and Mara had leisurely begun to furnish the cottage while Harve started advertising for tenants. She had not felt the need to rush to finish her task. Judging by the wide smile on Harve's face as he waited for her at the front door, she thought she might have been wrong.

"Hello, Harve." Her mouth curved in a polite reciprocation of his smile. "You said you had some good news. Is it about the cottage?"

She walked past him and opened the front door. Entering the house, she took it for granted that Harve would follow her—which he did.

"It's about the cottage," he answered. "I had a phone call from a man today who's interested in it."

The wide entry hall split the house in two. At the end, an L-shaped staircase that had once been enclosed led to the second floor. The sliding oak doors to the study, formerly the parlor, were open, hardwood floors glistening from beneath an area rug.

From inside that room on the left, Adam Prentiss called, "Was there any mail for me, Mara?"

"Yes." She paused and separated the envelopes addressed to her father from the others she had in her hand. "I'll only be a moment," she said to Harve and walked into the study. "Here you are." She placed the mail on the desk behind which her father's wheelchair was positioned.

He glanced beyond her to the man standing in the hallway. "Hello, Harve," he greeted him affably. "How's business?"

"We're selling a few houses," was the falsely modest response. "How are you, Mr. Prentiss?"

"Fine, fine," was Adam's dismissing reply, and he began looking through his mail.

As Mara turned to rejoin Harve, she let her gaze inspect his features. Cynically she thought that fresh-scrubbed, faintly freckled face had probably been responsible for selling quite a few houses. Although in his early thirties, Harve Bennett still possessed the wholesome innocence of a boy—a trick of nature, Mara was sure.

"Shall we go into the kitchen?" she suggested smoothly. Whatever Harve had come to discuss, it was no business of her father's. And she didn't want him listening in on their conversation.

"Sounds great. I could use a cup of coffee if you have any made," he said unabashedly.

"I think there's some left from lunch," she admitted, amused rather than irritated by his naturally pushy behavior.

Pushing open the swinging door to the kitchen, she walked to the coat rack. Harve was there to help her out of the wool jacket. She coolly smiled a thank-you before hanging the jacket on its hook.

"You said you had a phone call from someone interested in the cottage." She reminded him of the reason for his visit as she walked to the counter where the electric coffeepot was plugged in. "Someone local?"

"No, from Baltimore." Harve pulled one of the chairs away from the table and sat down, rocking it back on two legs and clasping his hands behind his head.

"From Baltimore? Why? Is this person moving here?" Mara filled two coffee mugs and carried them to the table. "Cream or sugar?"

"Haven't you remembered by now that I take it straight?" he chided her, and let all four legs of the chair come down on the floor with a resounding thud. "It seems your prospective tenant is looking for a weekend retreat so he can get away from the hassle of the city and the pressure of work."

"I suppose he wants to see it," she concluded logically. Sitting in one of the other chairs, she mentally began to calculate how long it might take her to complete furnishing the cottage if she devoted all of her spare time to it. "I have the bedroom furniture and the kitchen appliances there, as well as a sofa, but—"

"He doesn't want to see it," Harve interrupted.

"You don't mean he's going to rent it sight unseen?" Mara looked at him in frowning surprise.

"I didn't mean exactly that he isn't going to see it," Harve qualified his previous statement. "He can't get away right now and I, er—" he grinned "—gave him the impression that you already had several inquiries about the cottage and wouldn't be inclined to let it sit vacant until he was free to come here to look at it."

"So how is he going to see it?" she persisted.

"When I told him it was out in the country, secluded and quiet, he said it sounded like just what he was looking for. I almost got a commitment from him over the phone," said Harve, the pride in his selling ability surfacing with the claim. "To make sure he wasn't renting a log cabin instead of a cottage, and to speed things up, he wants me to send him some Polaroid pictures of it. I promised I'd send them to him in tomorrow's mail."

"Tomorrow? That's worse than I thought," she muttered. "Why did you do that, Harve? You know it isn't completely furnished yet."

"I told him that. He said he was only interested in the bare necessities." Harve sipped at his coffee, cradling the mug in both his hands.

It was all beginning to sound too good to be true. Mara felt a surge of skepticism that all wasn't as wonderful as Harve seemed to think.

"Who is this man? What do you know about him?" she demanded. "Is he young or old? After all the money I've spent fixing the cottage up, I'm not going to rent it to some wild young kids so they can wreck it partying all weekend."

"It's difficult to judge people over the telephone." he defended himself. "His name is Sinclair Buchanan. He sounded mature and well educated. I bumped the monthly rental a hundred dollars higher and he didn't even hesitate when I told him the price."

"A hundred dollars?" She was stunned.

"I thought that would get your attention." A smug smile curved his mouth.

"But why?" As far as Mara was concerned, the

price they had been going to charge would have allowed her an ample profit for the repairs.

"He sounded as if he could afford it," Harve shrugged. "If he squawked at it, I could always say I'd read it wrong. As it is, you stand to make a handsome profit."

His reasoning was logical even if Mara found his ethics questionable. She lifted the coffee mug to her mouth, refusing to be stampeded into something because of some dollar signs. She sipped at the coffee and set the mug down.

"Still, Harve, I'm not going to rent it to just anybody, regardless of how much money is involved."

"Don't worry, Mara. If, after he's seen the pictures of the cottage, he wants to sign a lease, I'm entitled to ask him for personal and credit references. I'll check Mr. Sinclair Buchanan out thoroughly," he promised.

"See that you do, because I'll want to see the results." Mara informed him, the tone of her voice carrying an underlying warning.

"We have to take first things first." Harve wasn't concerned by her lack of total confidence in him; he had an extraordinary amount of confidence in himself. "And the first thing I have to do is take those pictures I have to send to him. To do that, I need the key to the cottage."

"I'll get it for you." Mara rose from her chair.

Harve was instantly on his feet. His hand was on her arm when she started to walk past him. "Better yet, why don't you come with me while I take those photos?" He was standing slightly behind her, his low, coaxing voice coming from the general vicinity near her ear.

"I'm busy. Maybe another time." She coolly brushed aside his invitation and would have walked out of his light hold, but he tightened it at the last minute.

"You're always telling me 'another time,'" he protested.

Mara felt the warmth of his breath against the bare skin of her neck, exposed by the short, smooth style of her sable black hair. There was a fleeting irritation that if Harve was aware of the number of times she'd put him off, why hadn't he got the message?

"It simply isn't possible today." Her response was firm and unmoved by his veiled criticism.

There was an instant of silence, and Mara sensed that Harve was debating whether this was the moment to press the issue. Finally his grip on her arm loosened and he stepped away, chuckling softly.

"I don't know what there is about you, Mara," he commented. "With most girls, after the second refusal, I'd stop asking. But with you, I keep leaving myself open for rejection."

"I'll get the key to the cottage," she said.

"Is that all you have to say?" His exasperation was tinged with amusement. "Doesn't anything ruffle that cool composure of yours?"

Her lips curved in a semblance of a smile, but she didn't respond to his question. She doubted that Harve had really expected a reply. Leaving the kitchen, she walked to the study where she kept the key to the cottage in the desk drawer.

"Are you going to the cottage?" her father asked when she removed the key.

"I'm not. Harve has to go over to take some pictures for an out-of-town party who's interested in it." She took secret delight in relating the news to her father, considering his skepticism about the project.

"I thought it wasn't finished yet."

"All the repairs are done. It just isn't all furnished yet, but this person doesn't seem to mind," Mara explained. But she didn't mention the possibly higher rental income from the cottage. That was something she would keep to herself until a lease agreement was actually signed.

"Just make sure you know what type of person you're renting to," her father cautioned. "There's more to being a landlord than just collecting rent. There are those who tend to be destructive or careless with other people's property."

"I really don't need your advice, Adam," she retorted stiffly. "I've been handling my own affairs all by myself for quite some time. Virtually from the day you walked out."

He sighed. "I'm not trying to—"

"I know what you're trying to do," Mara interrupted with freezing contempt. "You may live in this house, but you won't control my life the way you controlled mother's."

She turned on her heel and swept out of the room. Harve waited in the kitchen. His gaze moved over her as she entered. Mara's arctic indifference to his caressive look made him take a deep breath of confused frustration.

"Here's the key." She handed it to him.

He looked at it for a second before his fingers closed around it. "I'll bring it back when I'm finished. It shouldn't take too long."

"All right," said Mara, since some kind of answer seemed to be expected of her.

"Are you sure you won't change your mind and come with me?" Harve tipped his head to one side, half expecting the answer he received.

"No."

"That's what I thought." A wry smile crooked his mouth. "See you later."

"Yes. Goodbye, Harve."

"And don't worry about the cottage or Sinclair Buchanan. I'll make sure it's a clean, sweet deal," he assured her with a wink. "Or we'll pass on it."

When Harve had gone, Mara lingered in the kitchen. The decision would be hers. She was not going to be influenced by Harve or money, and especially not by her father.

CHAPTER TWO

A WEEK LATER Harve telephoned to let Mara know that Sinclair Buchanan was definitely interested in leasing the cottage. A few days after that Harve came to the farmhouse with the references supplied by Buchanan.

"You see, he checks out," Harve declared triumphantly as Mara went over the information. "He's not only a solid citizen with impeccable personal references, but I'm almost embarrassed that I questioned his credit."

Mara studied the papers for a moment longer, almost wishing she could find something to fault. There was nothing, but she couldn't shake off the feeling of unease.

"It appears you're right," she agreed, however reluctantly.

"You could be a bit more enthusiastic," he grumbled. "This is a great deal, Mara. You're unbelievably lucky to get an offer like this for the cottage. It wouldn't hurt you to show a little excitement."

"I'm aware of my good fortune," Mara insisted, and stacked the pieces of paper neatly to return them to the folder. "I simply think it's wiser to wait until I see his signature on a lease agreement before I begin celebrating.''

"His signature and a check for the first and last months' lease payment. Don't forget that,'' Harve reminded her.

''I haven't forgotten,'' she assured him.

''In the meantime—'' he removed a folded document from the inner pocket of his suit jacket ''—let's get your signature on the agreement so I can forward it to Buchanan for his.''

He spread the printed form on the kitchen table and handed Mara a pen. She read it through before placing her signature of ''M. Prentiss'' on the line Harve indicated. When it was done Mara felt better, as if she had made some important decision. It was really quite ridiculous to feel that way. She had signed a simple lease agreement, hardly likely to change her life.

''Why look so worried?'' he chided. ''From this point on it's merely a formality.''

''I'm not worried,'' she denied.

As Harve had predicted, the final phases of the agreement proved to be a mere formality. The lease had been mailed to Sinclair Buchanan. By return mail Harve received Mara's copy with the lessee's signature affixed to it and a check. When he brought the document to the house, Mara guessed the reason for his visit by the expression on his face.

''Here it is.'' He produced the envelope with an air of self-satisfaction. ''All signed, sealed and delivered.''

On the last word, he handed it to her with a slight

flourish. Mara took it, removing the papers from the envelope and glancing at the signature scribbled across the line to be sure it was there. A cashier's check was clipped to the agreement. Mara glanced at the amount and raised a questioning eyebrow at Harve.

"This isn't the right amount. It's too much," she said.

"Yes, I know," he admitted, and gestured toward the papers she held. "There's a letter with it. Mr. Buchanan is driving up Friday evening. He sent a list of supplies he'd like stocked. That's why he sent the extra money—for supplies and any inconvenience his request has caused."

Mara found the letter and skimmed the list. It consisted of mainly staple food items with a few basic supplies. Her first impression was that his request was arrogantly presumptuous, but she conceded that he appeared willing to pay for this extra service.

"Mr. Buchanan is very generous," she observed, unable to keep the hint of asperity out of her voice.

"I thought it might be easier if you took care of the list," said Harve. "I could arrange for one of the girls at the office to handle it if you're too busy."

"I'll take care of it when I do my own shopping," she stated.

"That's what I thought, too," he smiled. "Another thing—I've made arrangements for him to come here to the house to pick up the key to the cottage. In his letter, he doesn't mention when he'll be arriving. Our office closes at five o'clock, so it seemed the most sensible thing to have him pick it up here."

"That's fine," Mara agreed, and folded the papers to return them to their envelope. "Mr. Buchanan and I will have to meet sometime. It might as well be when he moves in."

There was a nervous trembling in the region of her stomach. She blamed it on the fact that she had never been a landlady before. It was a new experience for her.

"I almost wish I'd rented the cottage so I could have you for a landlady. The problem is I couldn't afford the price," Harve grinned lazily.

"I doubt very seriously that you're poorly paid," Mara retorted.

His grin widened with boyish charm. "As a matter of fact, I didn't do too badly this month. With that check, neither have you." He pointed to the papers she held in her hand. "Why don't we celebrate? Have dinner with me Saturday night?"

Mara shook her head. "I'm afraid I can't, Harve. M—"

"If you say 'maybe another time,' so help me, I'll strangle you, Mara," Harve threatened insincerely. "This time I'm not going to let you turn me down without offering a legitimate reason."

"Harve...." She took a deep breath, determined to keep her patience.

"No, I mean it, Mara. Why can't you go out with me on Saturday night?" he demanded, the amusement leaving his expression.

"I can't leave Adam alone for that length of time," she stated.

"Your father is perfectly capable of looking after

himself for one evening. I asked you to have dinner with me, not the entire night," Harve pointed out.

"I don't agree with you. Adam shouldn't be left alone," Mara maintained stubbornly.

"I won't accept that." He caught her by the shoulders and kept her facing him when she would have turned away. "I can't make it much more obvious how I feel about you. I've been asking you out for months. I can't get you out of my head."

"Oh, please, Harve—" her look was cool in its amusement "—spare me those awful lines! You can't really expect me to believe them."

"It's the truth," he declared, anger surfacing that she should doubt him.

"And I suppose you were thinking of me while you've been dating all those other girls I've heard about. Let's see—there's that nurse at the hospital, the schoolteacher, a legal secretary." She began taunting him with the list of his most recent conquests.

"For God's sake, Mara, what do you expect from me?" He let her go and turned away, running a manicured hand through his carefully groomed dark brown hair.

"I don't expect anything from you." Which was the truth in many ways.

"I've been seeing other women," Harve admitted with an unconscious air of defensiveness. "Why shouldn't I? Whenever I'm around you, all I get is the cold shoulder. I happen to be human—even if you're not."

"If you have that opinion of me, then I don't

understand why you keep hanging around," Mara challenged.

"Do you know something?" Harve glared at her, his usually smiling mouth thinned into a grim line. "I don't know why I'm hanging around here, either. It's been a waste of time and effort for what would have probably turned out to be sour grapes anyway."

Mara felt no emotion as he stalked away. The slamming door seemed such a childish gesture that it drew a faintly contemptuous smile to her mouth. But the whir of the wheelchair wiped it from her face. She turned to meet the approach of her father.

"Harve left in something of a rush, didn't he?" he commented.

"He suddenly remembered an important appointment somewhere else," she returned.

"A sudden appointment?" His expression was skeptically mocking. "I thought it was probably a severe case of frostbite."

"Do you think it's cold in here?" Mara deliberately misunderstood his reference to her. "I'm quite comfortable myself. Maybe you should put on a sweater."

"I don't need one," Adam retorted wryly. "I've become acclimatized to the chill." His gaze noted the papers she held. "I suppose that's the cottage lease."

"Yes. Mr. Buchanan will be arriving Friday. Perhaps you'd like to look over the documents to make sure no one has taken advantage of me." She walked to his wheelchair and dropped the envelope in his lap.

Her attitude puzzled him until he looked at the

lease and saw the monthly rental fee. Triumph glittered in her eyes when Adam looked up.

"What do you think?" Mara challenged.

"It's excellent." He handed the papers back to her. "I'm just wondering how you did it."

"Maybe it's one of the financial rewards of good, clean living," she suggested with a trace of sarcasm for the way he was always mocking her for being too righteous.

His dark head moved as he exhaled a wryly amused breath. "Were you properly grateful to Harve for signing this deal? Or did you show him the door because he'd served his purpose and you no longer had any use for him?"

Mara stiffened. "Harve is aware that I give him full credit for arranging the terms of the lease. Our relationship has always been purely a business one. I'm not obliged to have dinner with him just because the deal was concluded satisfactorily."

"Poor Harve," Adam mused. "I should have warned him that gods don't mingle socially with us mortals."

Mara was almost overwhelmed by an impulse to scream at her father to stop ridiculing her, but she fought it down to reply coldly, "I wouldn't worry about Harve. He already shares your opinion that I'm not human."

He held her gaze for a long moment. Some kind of silent appeal gleamed from the depths of his brown eyes, but Mara couldn't fathom it and didn't try.

Sighing, he turned his chair and changed the subject. "So on Friday you officially assume the role of landlady."

"Yes," Mara automatically stepped forward to push the chair toward the study. "I'll be going into town Friday afternoon to pick up the items Mr. Buchanan requested. If there's anything you need while I'm there, let me know."

"How about a loving daughter?" he responded in a low, weary voice.

"You had one once." She didn't elaborate further. He knew the rest.

FRIDAY AFTERNOON Mara separated the grocery bags, leaving the ones destined for the cottage in the rear of the station wagon, and carried the rest into the house. The grandfather clock in the entry hall chimed the half hour. It was after three, later than she had realized. Hurriedly she began removing the perishable items from the grocery bags and storing them in the refrigerator.

The door to the kitchen swung open to admit her father's wheelchair. "You're running late, aren't you?" he observed.

"Yes." Mara didn't pause in her task. "Did Mr. Buchanan arrive while I was gone?"

"No."

"Do you have the key to the cottage?" She had left it with him before she'd gone to town.

"Right here." He produced it from the pocket of his cranberry sweater, a color that intensified his dark good looks.

Mara put the lettuce in the crisper and the cheese

on the refrigerator shelf, the last of the items. Taking
the key from her father, she walked to the back door.

"I'm going to the cottage. If Mr. Buchanan arrives
before I come back, send him down by the back
trail," she instructed.

"Will do," he agreed as Mara went out of the
door.

The red brick farmhouse sat on one hundred acres
of wooded Pennsylvania land. The previous owner
had cleared and farmed two hundred acres adjoining
this property, intending someday to clear the rest of
the woods. When Mara's father had bought the place
some twenty years ago, he had sold off the farmland
but kept the wooded land that surrounded the house.
A neighboring farmer now leased the bulk of it to
graze his cattle.

The cottage was located in the far corner of the
property. There were two ways of reaching it. One
was a graveled lane that led to the country road. The
second was a dirt track that wound through the trees
to the farmhouse. In bad weather, the latter was
sometimes impassable, but that wasn't the case today.

The station wagon thumped across the cattle
guard, which, along with a fence, kept the neighbor's
cattle from straying into the house yard. The autumn
scarlet of the sumac lined the way. A thin carpet of
gold and brown fallen leaves covered the trail, rus-
tling and whirling as Mara drove slowly along. Overhead the trees had exploded with color, most of the
leaves still clinging tenaciously to the branches.

It was a gorgeous Indian summer afternoon with

cloudless blue sky and briskly invigorating air. The heavily ribbed turtleneck sweater of ivory wool was all Mara needed in the mild temperature of this September day. The pale color drew attention to the silky black of her hair and complemented the forest green plaid of her slacks.

Rounding a curve, she glimpsed the cottage through the trees. Where a second fence line intersected the trail was another cattle guard. Mara slowed the car as she crossed the iron grate and parked in front of the cottage.

The slanted roof of the low building was covered with shake shingles. The exterior siding was stained cedar and the windows and doors were trimmed with a burnt shade of rust. The cottage blended in appearance with its woodsy setting.

Balancing a bag of groceries on her hip, Mara unlocked the front door and walked into the living room, dominated by a large, native stone fireplace. The sparse furnishings didn't do justice to the potential of the room.

To the left was the kitchen and Mara's destination. All the birch cabinets had been stripped and restained, and the counter tops resurfaced. A small table and chairs occupied the breakfast nook and shiny copper pots hung above the stove. The atmosphere was distinctly warm and homey. Mara set the one bag down and went back to the car for the others.

The third and last room of the cottage was the bedroom with a full bath off it. Mara didn't classify the small utility room as a room since it was little more than a large closet.

Despite possessing only three rooms, the cottage gave the impression of spaciousness. But Mara didn't have time to admire its efficient design. All the supplies and food had to be put away.

The last bag was half-emptied when Mara thought she heard the sound of a car out front. She paused to listen and heard the slam of a car door. Leaving the can of coffee sitting on the counter, she made a detour on the way to the front door, stopping to glance out the kitchen window for an advance look at the cottage's new occupant. She had a brief glimpse of a tall, gray-haired gentleman approaching the front door before he disappeared out of her angle of sight.

Reassured somehow by the sight of that gray hair, Mara had barely straightened from the window when there came a loud knock at the door. Unconsciously she squared her shoulders and lifted her chin to a lofty angle. The familiar aloofness settled over her as she went to answer the knock.

When she was opening the door, her mouth automatically curved into a detached smile of greeting. Her gaze first encountered the towering bulk of the man outside, then met a pair of smoky blue eyes. Her expression froze in place. Tiny shock waves disassembled her previous image of the man and threw it away.

This was not some old, distinguished gentleman facing her. This was a rawly virile man, suntanned and vigorous. The civilized impression given by the tweed jacket and dark trousers was banished by the unbuttoned shirt and the hard, browned flesh it revealed. The fact that his thick mane of hair happened to be iron gray was purely incidental.

All the while she was staring at him, he was studying her in an odd way, as if she wasn't what he had expected to see, either. Maybe there was some kind of mistake. Mara clutched at that straw.

"Mr. Buchanan?" she questioned.

"Yes." There was the faintest inclination of his head to affirm his identity. "I stopped at the farmhouse and Mr. Prentiss sent me down here. Are you his daughter?"

The soothing pitch of his low voice was strangely unsettling, but Mara didn't betray her feelings. Instead she drew her invisible cloak of aloofness more tightly around her.

"Yes, I am. Mara Prentiss." The introduction seemed to demand a perfunctory handshake.

She offered him hers and found her slim fingers swallowed up in the grip of his. She didn't like the sensation of being engulfed by his sheer physical presence. It was somehow diminishing. Her temperature dropped by several degrees as she withdrew her hand from his grasp.

There was a lift of detached amusement to his mouth. "For some reason, I expected to meet your father's wife or sister."

"My mother is dead." Mara didn't know why she offered the information.

"Mara Prentiss. M. Prentiss?" He referred to the signature on the lease.

"The same," she admitted, stiffly holding herself erect as if she needed every centimeter of stature.

Behind the cloud blue of his eyes, there seemed to be a wicked light dancing. Mara thought she had glimpsed it a couple of times previously, and it gave her the impression of danger rather than mischief. It was like that opaque gleam in the eyes of a cat playing with its prey.

"I presume everything is in order for my arrival," he prompted.

And Mara realized she was still barring his entrance into the cottage. "Yes, it is." She stepped back to admit him. "I was just putting away the supplies you ordered."

One gleaming shoe had just crossed the threshold when a female voice halted him. "Sin, darling, shall I bring any of the luggage when I come?"

Mara's gaze jerked beyond him to the sleek gray car parked next to her station wagon. A stunning redhead was just stepping out of the passenger side. Her white silk blouse was unbuttoned to show off her cleavage while a pair of midnight-blue slacks tightly hugged her hips. Despite the suggestiveness of her attire, the overall impression was one of chic sophistication.

"Leave it," was his answer. "I'll carry it in later."

Tearing her gaze away from the scarlet-haired beauty, Mara let it touch briefly on the man entering the cottage. Sinclair Buchanan, aptly shortened to Sin, she concluded without being sure why.

Mara blamed her brief start of surprise at the presence of the woman on two things. All her attention had been focused on Sinclair Buchanan, so any distraction would have caught her off guard. The sec-

ond was the length of time the woman had waited
before making her presence known. Mara would
have thought that she would have accompanied him
to the door. Most wives would have exhibited more
curiosity or been more eager to see their newly leased
cottage.

Sinclair Buchanan was inside now and Mara re-
directed her attention to him. Aware that this was the
first time he'd seen the cottage other than in photo-
graphs, she felt she should make some attempt to
familiarize him with the place.

"This, of course, is the living room," she stated
the obvious. He was already making a slow, sweeping
survey of the interior. Mara couldn't tell by his expression whether he was disappointed by what he saw
or not, but she felt she should offer some excuse for
the starkness of the room. "As Mr. Bennett told you,
the cottage isn't completely furnished. If you wish,
I—"

"No, I'll see to the rest of it myself." He refused
her offer to finish decorating the place before she had
had a chance to complete it. "Is the fireplace
usable?"

"Yes. The chimney has been swept and the flues
checked," she assured him. "As a matter of fact,
Mr. Bennett and I had a fire going in it just a few
weeks ago to be certain there was no problem."

The touch of his gaze gave her the impression that
he had put a romantic connotation on her elaboration. In actual fact, there had been workers around
finishing up the repairs, but she felt no compulsion to
explain further.

"What about firewood?" he questioned.

"There's some wood stacked behind the cottage. You're welcome to gather the deadfall in the woods, but not to cut down any trees," she told him.

Instantly she visualized him stripped to the waist against a backdrop of woods, splitting logs for the fireplace. She could even picture the sheen of perspiration glistening over the powerful muscles of his arms and chest. The image prompted a sudden surge of life to throb through her veins, which unnerved her because she couldn't control it.

In unconscious self-defense, she turned away from him to break the crazy spell. As she did, the redhead walked through the open door. Mara smiled as if it had been her intention all along to greet the woman just entering the cottage, but the woman didn't even glance at her.

The redhead's brown eyes were alight with excitement as she made an inspecting circle of the living room. When she came to a stop beside Sinclair Buchanan, her expression was alive with delight and anticipation. She circled one of his arms with both of hers and hugged him.

"It's charming, Sin," she declared. "So rustic and quaint! Can't you picture an old sofa in front of the fireplace? We'll have such fun decorating this place."

His look was indulgent, as if faintly amused, as he gazed at the upturned face of the woman. Fiery clouds of scarlet hair fell loosely around her shoulders. Mara was beginning to feel superfluous.

"Be honest, Celene. You're just looking forward

to spending my money." His tone fell halfway between teasing and taunting, as large a difference as
between love and cruelty. His true attitude was a
matter of interpretation.

With a mock pout, the woman named Celene
chose the first interpretation. Mara wasn't in a position to argue with the decision. Celene was obviously
better acquainted with this man's moods and meaning than she was.

"You know that isn't true, Sin," the redhead
denied. "I enjoy spending *anybody*'s money." She
laughed. "I pride myself on being totally impartial.
Come on, let's see the rest of the cottage."

Before replying, his gaze swung to Mara. There
was something prompting in his look. Mara didn't
know what it was that he wanted, so she left it up to
him to explain.

"Shall I show you through the cottage or would
you prefer to explore on your own?" she inquired.

"We'll find our way around. I don't think we'll get
lost," he assured her in a dry voice.

"I should hope not!" Celene laughed at the comment that Mara had found more cutting than amus-
ing.

"If you'll excuse me," she murmured coolly, I'll
finish putting the groceries away." She paused to
glance at the redhead. "Unless you would prefer to
do—"

"Please go ahead, Miss Prentiss." It was Sinclair Buchanan who answered. Mara couldn't help
wondering if he made a habit of interrupting. His
gaze slid down to the woman on his arm. "Celene

is helpless—or should I say hopeless—in the kitchen."

The woman smiled at the taunting observation. "Sin knows me," she sighed, and turned her soft brown eyes on Mara. "But then I've never claimed that my talents were in that area."

"I'm sure you're very good at whatever you do." Mara's response was merely polite words, a murmured reply to be taken at face value.

It drew a low chuckle from Sinclair Buchanan that earned him a playful slap of reprimand from the redhead. Celene's "talents" were obviously a private and intimate joke between them, and Mara wanted no further part in it. Turning quietly, she walked into the kitchen.

The cottage was too small for her not to hear the murmuring of their voices as the couple wandered from the living room to the bedroom. She tried to drown out the sound with the whir of the electric can opener on the can of coffee.

Pouring a portion of the grounds into the coffee canister, she set the rest inside the cupboard. She had just lifted the bag of flour out of the grocery bag when the two entered the kitchen.

"This is your province, Sin. I'll leave you to inspect it," the red-haired Celene declared. "There's something I want to get from the car. I'll only be a moment."

As the woman departed, Mara was conscious of Sin Buchanan remaining in the kitchen. She opened the flap of the flour bag and reached for the canister. As she emptied the flour into it, she was aware of his movements, checking the appliances and the cupboards. His silvered gray hair was like a beacon.

"I bought everything you had on the list," Mara informed him as she pushed the canister into its position with the rest of the set, "I hope you won't have difficulty finding anything."

"I doubt it," he replied. "Everything appears well organized." It was an observation rather than a compliment.

The dumping of the bag had left a fine film of flour dust on the counter, and Mara dampened a dishcloth to wipe it away. While she finished up in the kitchen, her new tenant wandered back into the living room. His return coincided with the entrance of Celene. There was nothing to keep their voices from carrying into the kitchen.

"I found the wineglasses, so I brought in the champagne to toast the new cottage," Celene's voice announced in husky invitation. "The ice cooler chilled it to perfection. Here, open it, Sin."

An assortment of spices and herbs was at the bottom of the grocery bag. Mara tried to remain deaf to the conversation in the adjoining room as she began arranging the bottles on the spice rack.

"Don't you want to leave the celebrating until later?" The pop of the champagne cork made his question insignificant.

But Celene answered it anyway. "No, I want to start now." Her voice was a throaty purr. "This is the first weekend I've ever had you all to myself. No phone calls, no business, *no* interruptions." The last negative was emphatically stressed. Celene proposed the toast, "To our first weekend alone."

It was followed by the clinking of crystal and then silence. An inner voice seemed to order Mara to keep quiet and not betray her presence in the cottage, but she refused to obey it. The bottles thudded onto the spice shelf with the same regularity.

"Mmmm, you know what let's do tonight, darling," Celene answered her own question without giving Sin a chance to respond. "Build a roaring fire in the fireplace. Then we'll lie down in front of it and...." The rest of her suggestion was made in a whisper.

Mara's stomach knotted into a tight ball of nerves. The entire situation was making her irritated and on edge. A can of dried parsley flakes was the last item in the grocery bag. She shoved it quickly into place and folded up the paper bag, stowing it beneath the sink.

In the opening to the living room, Mara hesitated. The couple were in front of the fireplace, locked in a kiss. Celene's arms were wound around Sin's neck while she still managed to hold the champagne glass. One of his hands was on her rib cage, almost cupping her breast. His other arm was pressed against the small of her back, arching the redhead to his muscled body. That hand held his glass. Neither had apparently spilled any champagne in the process since there was liquid in each of the glasses.

Mara started to retreat into the kitchen until this passionate embrace was over, but she stopped herself. Why should she scurry off as if their kissing made her uncomfortable? If anyone was going to feel awkward from her intrusion, let it be them, she decided. She took another step into the living room.

"Excuse me, I'm leaving now," she announced with composure, her voice cool.

With remarkable aplomb and absence of haste, they untangled themselves from each other without tipping their champagne glasses. Celene smoothed the fiery strands of hair from her cheek in a self-conscious gesture, but there was a pleasantly satisfied gleam in her eyes, especially when they darted to Sin.

"I'm sorry, Miss Prentiss," she apologized while he sipped at his champagne. "I'm afraid we got a bit carried away."

Secretly Mara thought that excuse might be true for Celene, but a glance at the woman's partner made her doubt that it had been equally true of him. He looked fully in control of himself and his passions.

"There's no need to apologize." Her mouth curved, but it wasn't much of a smile.

Sinclair Buchanan moved, drawing Mara's gaze. His sports jacket was unbuttoned, the front held open by the hand thrust in the pocket of his slacks. That casual air was a pose; Mara realized that he was every bit as alert as she was.

"I haven't thanked you for ensuring that we have something to eat this weekend," he said.

"It isn't necessary, Mr. Buchanan," Mara countered. "You've already amply compensated me." Before she made her departure, courtesy demanded that she add, "I hope you find the cottage to your satisfaction. If you or your wife have any questions, please contact me."

Celene broke into a laugh and immediately covered

her mouth, her brown gaze dancing to Sin. "Darling, she thinks we're married!"

"Yes." His amusement was more distant as he turned and lifted an inquiring eyebrow at the red-head. "I wonder where she got that idea...."

Mara's chin tipped to an angle a scant degree higher than before, the only outward sign of her recoiling shock. She had wrongly presumed the couple were married. She was reluctant to make another assumption in case it should be wrong, too.

"It's my fault, Miss Prentiss." Sin took the blame without exhibiting any remorse for his action. "I failed to introduce Celene when we arrived. Miss Prentiss, this is Celene Taylor, a friend of mine. Celene, Mara Prentiss," he corrected the oversight.

"How do you do, Miss Taylor." Mara acknowledged the introduction stiffly and received a smiling nod in return.

"Celene is spending the weekend with me," he stated. "I don't recall seeing any restriction in the lease against having friends visit."

"Of course, there was none," Mara admitted disliking his baiting tone. "But you do realize there's only one bedroom," she reminded him coldly, and immediately wished she hadn't said it.

That devilish glint was back in his eyes. "Yes, I do know, Miss Prentiss. It is Miss isn't it?" Again he jibed at her naiveté.

"Yes, it is." Mara tried desperately not to snap out the answer. The only way out of this mess seemed to be a dignified retreat. "I know you'll want to bring your luggage in and get unpacked, so I won't keep you any longer. Good day, Mr. Buchanan...Miss Taylor."

Mara turned toward the door only to be halted by a low male voice. "Miss Prentiss, aren't you forgetting something?"

She glanced over her shoulder, her look totally blank. "I beg your pardon? Forgetting what?"

"The key to the cottage," Sin replied. "I believe I need one."

Silently calling herself fifty kinds of a fool, Mara reached into the pocket of her slacks and took out the key. Sin Buchanan walked over to take it from her. She practically dropped it in her haste to give it to him.

Her eyes blazed at the amused curl of his mouth. That opaque gleam was in his smoke-blue eyes playing over her face. Mara had never felt so impotent in her life. There was nothing she could do to change it.

"Thank you." His strong fingers closed around the key.

Mara nodded dumbly and pivoted toward the door. Rigidly she kept her steps unhurried as she exited from the cottage. She was trembling by the time she reached the station wagon.

CHAPTER THREE

By THE TIME Mara reached the house, her seething resentment had been controlled to a low simmer. Sinclair Buchanan had made her look a fool. She didn't like that—nor him. She should have known her new tenant sounded too good to be true. Why had she listened to Harve and rented the cottage without first meeting the man?

Not that it would have made any difference, Mara concluded as she walked to the back door of the red brick house. "Sin darling" probably wouldn't have brought his mistress to that meeting. Not that she cared whether he had a mistress, she reminded herself. But the pair of them, mostly Sin, had made her look so damn prudish. And she wasn't. She didn't care how other people behaved.

Slamming the back door, she tossed the car keys on the kitchen counter. They slid against a grocery bag. Mara was reminded that none of this would have happened if she hadn't taken so long in town getting the supplies. His groceries would have been put away and she would have been here to give him the key when he stopped for it, then she wouldn't have been subjected to the embarrassing incident.

"Mara?" Her father entered the kitchen. Immediately she began unpacking the rest of their groceries. "That Buchanan fellow stopped here. I sent him down to the cottage. Did you see him?"

"Yes," she answered without elaboration.

"How did they like the cottage?" he inquired. "I caught a glimpse of his wife in the car. From what I could tell, she looked to be a strikingly beautiful woman, but not exactly the type for a cottage in the Pennsylvania woods."

"She loved it." Mara sarcastically stressed the verb, the woman's gushy "Sin darling" echoing in her mind. "But she isn't his wife."

Her voice was hard and flat as she made the announcement. She continued to stack the canned goods in the cupboard without a break in her rhythm, but there was a hint of angry agitation in her movements.

"Not his wife?" Adam Prentiss echoed in an initially blank voice. "You mean...." He began chuckling to himself as he realized what she meant. "I suppose it was a natural mistake." Mara said nothing, not admitting it was a mistake she had made, too. "There's nothing like bringing your own entertainment along with you to while away the hours."

"*Must* you be so disgustingly crude!" Mara slammed the cupboard door shut. An image of her new tenant and his mistress cuddling in front of the fireplace leaped into her mind. It grated at the raw edge of her nerves, inflaming them again.

Her outburst was greeted by a moment of silence. When her father spoke, all trace of amusement was gone from his voice. His tone was serious and gently reprimanding.

"Sex isn't crude, Mara. It's a very beautiful thing."

"I don't care to hear any lecture from you on the subject!" she snapped.

A long sigh came from behind her, followed by the turning of the wheelchair. When the swinging door had slowly ended its pendulum movement, Mara was alone in the kitchen. Her hands were gripping the edges of the counter, her knuckles white.

For the rest of that day and all of Saturday, she blocked the cottage and its inhabitants from her mind. On Sunday morning she rose early as was her custom. While the coffee perked, she walked out to the mailbox for the Sunday newspaper. Her father was awake when she returned. After helping him into his robe, she held the wheelchair steady as he levered himself out of the bed into his chair.

The whole routine seemed timed to coincide with the moment the coffee had finished perking. It emitted its last popping sound as Mara wheeled her father into the kitchen. In silence they shared a glass of orange juice and a cup of fresh coffee before Mara fixed their breakfast of ham and eggs and hot rolls.

With the morning meal over, she stacked the dishes in the sink and filled it with hot, sudsy water. Her father's wheelchair remained positioned at the table while he read the newspaper and sipped a cup of coffee.

Mechanically Mara began washing the dishes. One

by one she washed them, rinsed them and stacked them on the draining board to dry. Her mind seemed blank as she performed the task, her gaze straying out the window above the sink to the woods beyond.

A large patch of blue caught her eye, and focusing on it, she saw a figure coming up the rutted trail from the cottage. It was Sin Buchanan, dressed in a sky-blue jogging suit. A black stripe ran down the long length of the legs. His muscled frame moved in effortless, athletic strides. The premature gray of his hair was at odds with the rest of him, a perfect male specimen in the prime of his manhood.

Mara watched him cross the cattle guard and approach the house at an easy, jogging pace. She expected him to turn up the driveway toward the graveled country road, and an alarm jangled through her nerves as she realized his destination was the vicinity of the back door.

In a sudden spurt of activity she began washing the dishes at a faster rate. Then a knock at the back door brought a stiffening of her spine, and the newspaper rustled as her father set it aside.

"I wonder who that could be," he murmured.

"I'll see." Mara avoided his questioning gaze as she dried her sudsy hands with a terry towel.

She walked to the door, steeling her features to be expressionless. When she opened it, Sin Buchanan stood outside, as she had known he would. His relaxed stance indicated that he felt totally at ease. Mara felt a fluttering tension in her stomach.

The even rise and fall of his broad chest revealed that the long jog from the cottage to the house had not left him winded. Her gaze lifted to his face and met the smoky blue of his eyes. They seemed somehow shuttered, his inner thoughts hidden from her. If anything, his eyes only reflected the coolness of her attitude. Her gaze flicked to his steel-gray hair that was so strangely in keeping with the dynamic thrust of his vitality.

"Good morning, Miss Prentiss." There was a sardonic lilt to his low-pitched voice.

"Was there something you needed, Mr. Buchanan?" Mara skipped the greeting to demand a reason for his appearance.

"Yes, there is." A faint light gleamed in his eyes, deriding her for asking a perfectly obvious question.

From behind her came Adam's voice. "Don't stand there with the door open, Mara—it's creating a draft. Invite him in."

The sheer practicality of the suggestion couldn't be ignored, as much as Mara wished that it could be. Her fingers tightened around the doorknob. Her impulse was to step outside to speak to him privately, without her father listening in, rather than to invite Sin Buchanan inside the house.

But there was a nip in the autumn morning. The warmth of Sin's breath was making a vaporous cloud in the outside air. Mara realized that if she attempted to conduct this conversation out of doors she would soon be shivering. The last thing she wanted to do was attempt to discuss business with her teeth chattering.

Reluctantly Mara swung the door wide to admit

him. "Please come in, Mr. Buchanan." There was little welcome in her voice. Mostly it held a grudging tolerance for his presence.

"Thank you." His response, too, was merely a polite expression without a foundation in sincerity. "I hope I'm not intruding."

As far as Mara was concerned, he was a definite intrusion and she had no intention of denying it. Unfortunately her father was inclined otherwise.

"Of course you're not, Mr. Buchanan," Adam insisted. "We've already had breakfast. Mara was just washing the dishes while I finished reading the paper. There is some coffee left, isn't there, Mara? Why don't you offer Mr. Buchanan a cup?"

She sent her father a silencing look. "I'm sure Mr. Buchanan has already had his morning coffee." Her glance challenged Sin to dispute her claim.

The amused slant of his mouth lacked humor. "As a matter of fact, I didn't take time for coffee before I left the cottage."

"Pour the gentleman a cup, Mara," her father instructed.

"All that's left is the bottom of the pot," she added a last warning, irritated that Sin Buchanan was taking advantage of the hospitality he must guess she didn't wish to extend.

"I like my coffee strong and black," he informed her, and glanced at her father. "Thank you for offering, Mr. Prentiss," expressing his gratitude to whom it was due.

"Sit down." Her father waved a hand to indicate a chair at the table. "And please call me Adam. With you staying at the cottage, you're virtually our closest neighbor, and I've never liked formality between neighbors."

"Neither have I," was the agreement. "I didn't introduce myself on Friday. Sinclair Buchanan," he identified himself, and shook hands with Adam before sitting in one of the chairs.

Having emptied the coffeepot into a mug, Mara carried it to the table and set it in front of him. "I believe your friends call you Sin, don't they?" Her subtle jibe was followed by the thought, *Sin by name and sin by nature.*

His blue eyes glanced up at her, challenge lurking in their steely depths. "That's correct," he admitted.

Immediately her remark seemed churlish. "You said you liked your coffee black?" She sought his affirmation to cover her previous words.

"Yes, thank you." The frosted gray hair inclined briefly in affirmation, something vaguely condescending in the action. As Sin lifted the mug to sip the scalding hot coffee, his gaze was directed at her father. "Adam Prentiss—I have the feeling I should know that name."

Adam had been studying his daughter. At the questioning remark addressed to him, he brought his attention back to the man at the table.

"I'm something of a local historian," he offered in explanation.

"Adam is being falsely modest," Mara inserted. "He's a very well known Civil War historian."

"That's where I've heard your name, then." Sin absorbed the information Mara supplied but ignored the acid sting in her voice. "A close friend of mine is an avid Civil War buff, and your name probably came up in our conversation."

Mara felt a curiosity for the identity of his friend and heard herself inquire skeptically, "Miss Taylor?" His red-haired mistress didn't seem the type to her.

"No." Sardonic amusement danced in his eyes while the rest of Sin's strong features remained smoothly expressionless. "A close *male* friend of mine."

Mara had the distinct impression that she had walked into a trap he had neatly set for her, and she didn't like the feeling. Sin Buchanan was an irritating and offensive man. She wished she could stop rising to his bait and learn to ignore it.

He was speaking again, this time to Adam. "I believe John mentioned your name as the author of a book he'd recently read about the Battle of Gettysburg."

"That's possible," her father conceded with a faint smile. "I have written one on the subject. It's a comfort to know someone has read it and it isn't gathering dust on the library shelves."

"I confess that I know very little about the battle or the Civil War." But Sin Buchanan wasn't apologizing for his ignorance or previous lack of interest.

"When the South lost the Battle of Gettysburg, they virtually lost the war even though it dragged on for another two years," Adam explained the significance of the battle in history.

"I don't think Mr. Buchanan is interested in hearing a lecture on it." Mara stated before her father could warm to his favorite subject. She turned a challenging look toward the blandly guarded expression of her tenant. "You said there was something you wanted to speak to me about, Mr. Buchanan?" She pointedly reminded him of the reason for his visit.

The slashing lines that ran from nose to mouth became more pronounced. Behind his lazy regard, Mara sensed he was laughing at her, silently, cynically. It heightened her feeling of antagonism toward him.

"Yes, there is," Sin admitted. "I want to make arrangements to have someone to clean the cottage on a weekly basis and have it in readiness for my weekend visits."

"I see," she murmured, and waited for him to continue.

"Since I'm new to the area, I thought you might recommend a responsible person for the job," he explained.

She couldn't argue with his logical request, but neither could she fulfill it. "Offhand, I can't think of anyone," she shrugged.

"Perhaps I can impose on you to find someone," he suggested. "It's difficult to conduct interviews long-distance, as well as time-consuming."

Silently Mara wished that he wasn't so damned logical. She wanted to disagree with him, but his proposal made too much sense.

"I'm flattered that you should trust my judgment." The ring of sarcasm in her voice eliminated the pleasure implied by her words.

"We both have a vested interest in ensuring that the cottage is well kept. Since you own it, you wouldn't want to see the property neglected, while I want to enjoy it in comfort," Sin reasoned with equitable calm.

"I quite agree." Mara paused to control the sharpness of her tongue. "But you must understand the difficulty in finding a reliable person who'll be willing to come so far out of the way. We're located off the beaten track."

Her comment didn't elicit an immediate response. Mara watched as Sin lifted the coffee mug to his firmly defined mouth. His large hand encircled the mug, a healthy tan coloring his skin. She felt her tension building from the volatile undercurrents rippling through the air. Her gaze strayed past Sin to her father, who was observing the subtly charged byplay between them with growing interest. Adam's presence aggravated the situation.

"I am aware it may not be easy, Miss Prentiss." Sin replaced the mug on the table, the fingers of both hands encircling it. He studied the mug for a moment before sliding his veiled gaze to her. "Naturally I'm more than willing to compensate you for your services."

"Naturally," she countered dryly. It seemed money was never an object where he was concerned.

"In the meantime, I'll need someone to look after the place while I'm gone during the week. I don't know whether it's proper to ask my landlady to do it or not, but you're conveniently close to the cottage." His mouth quirked in a half smile. "If you could spare the time to clean it after I leave and make sure it's aired and relatively well stocked with supplies before I arrive, I would greatly appreciate it."

Mara hesitated as she considered the alternatives. If she refused, there was the risk of dirt and dust collecting to the point where the cottage would need a major cleaning. Considering the time, money and effort she had put into it to this point, it would be foolish to let it get into a state of neglect.

"I can temporarily look after the cottage while I look for a reliable person to take over the duty," she agreed without realizing that her tone of voice made it sound as if she was doing him an enormous favor.

"Thank you, Miss Prentiss." Sin expressed his gratitude in a decidedly mocking way.

A surge of irritation was stifled with an effort. "I'll need to know what qualifications you're seeking in a housekeeper."

"You would know more about that than I do," he shrugged.

"What are you willing to pay, then?" Mara questioned.

"Whatever is fair. Perhaps you could make a suggestion on that." He put the question back to her.

"As long as the cottage isn't left in too much of a mess, it shouldn't require more than a couple of hours to clean and dust the rooms on a Monday. About the same amount of time would be needed on

Friday to air it and be certain whatever supplies you requested would be on hand." Mara voiced her thoughts aloud, sliding in a coolly subtle reprimand that he shouldn't leave the cottage too cluttered and dirty. "With traveling expenses back and forth from town, I should think fifty dollars a week would be a fair salary. Would you be willing to pay that, Mr. Buchanan?"

"I don't quibble over prices," he informed her with a distantly amused light in his eyes. "As long as I get what I want, I'm not concerned about the cost."

His supreme confidence grated at Mara. The carriage of her head became more stiffly erect and her attitude more withdrawn. "Very well, that's the salary I shall quote. Was there anything else?" Rising from her chair, she indicated by her action that if there was nothing, he should leave.

"No, that was all. Thanks for the coffee." Releasing the mug from the encirclement of his hands, Sin indolently uncoiled his length to dominate her with his height.

"There's no need to rush off," her father protested amiably.

The dark fires in her eyes smoldered in her father's direction as Mara curved her mouth into a false smile. "I'm sure Mr. Buchanan is aware that by now Miss Taylor is probably wondering where he disappeared to."

"Celene was sleeping when I left," Sin offered the information unasked. "She isn't an early riser. She'll probably still be in bed when I get back and I'll have to wake her."

Mara had an immediate mental picture of just how Sin would go about it. An unreasoning anger stabbed through her and she felt herself bristling because of it.

"No doubt she'll be pleased," she murmured sarcastically, and moved toward the door to escort Sin out.

But Sin didn't immediately follow her as he paused to say goodbye to her father. "I enjoyed meeting you, Adam."

"The pleasure was mine. As you can see, I don't get out much." Her father patted the armrest of his wheelchair, indicating his condition without asking for pity. "But I hope you find time to stop by for a visit again."

"Thank you. I'll try." His glance at Mara said that he was aware she didn't echo the invitation. "Good day, Miss Prentiss."

There was controlled amusement in the warmth of his resonant voice. It taunted her into offering a stilted, "Good day, Mr. Buchanan," as she opened the door for him.

His wide-shouldered bulk moved past her, his laconic strength evident in the ease of his long strides. Mara caught a whiff of some exotic male fragrance mixed with tobacco smoke. Then he was out of the door.

She closed the door, but it wasn't so easy to shut out his existence from her mind. Turning, she walked back to the sink and the now lukewarm dishwater. Through the window she could see Sin effortlessly jogging back the way he had come.

"I don't want you to encourage him to make social calls here, Adam," she stated, recalling her father's parting invitation. "I want the relationship to remain strictly landlord and tenant minus needless personal complications."

"I'm sure Sin is aware of your views," he replied in a dryly exasperated tone.

"I don't want you making friends with him, Adam," Mara restated her demand.

"You've never been concerned about who my friends are before. Why this sudden insistence that Sin Buchanan should not be among them?" Adam was both puzzled and intensely curious.

"I told you." She didn't look up from the skillet she was cleaning. "He's a tenant. Business and friendship don't mix."

"There's no business involved—at least, not between Sin and myself. He leases the cottage from you, not me," he reminded her. "So that argument doesn't stand up."

"Yes, I leased him the cottage," Mara snapped, "but I don't want him in this house!"

A slow half smile spread across her father's mouth. "He bothers you, doesn't he?" He tipped his head to one side, studying her in a considering manner.

"I don't know what you mean." She turned the tap on full force to rinse the soapsuds from the skillet.

"No," he replied and then paused. "Probably you don't."

Mara didn't want to explore the reasons behind

that remark. "What are you going to do if Sinclair Buchanan comes here again?" she demanded.

"He's my neighbor. If he comes, I'll invite him in," Adam stated.

"You'd do that after what I've just asked you?" She turned on him roundly.

"I not only would, but given the chance,.I will," he declared in open challenge.

"This happens to be my house," Mara reminded him in a cold voice.

"Sin Buchanan would be my guest. I've always invited whatever friends I pleased into this house in the past. You've never objected to who came to see me before—why are you making an exception with Sin?" There was a certain shrewd gleam in his dark eyes that Mara didn't like.

"The circumstances are different," she said in rigid defense of her reasons.

"No, they aren't," Adam denied that. "Besides, half the time when someone comes over to see me, you're off in some other room. If and when Sin ever comes here, you can go and hide in another part of the house until he leaves."

"Hide?" Her anger nearly boiled over, but she checked herself in time to insist acidly, "I'm not afraid of him."

"No?" A dark eyebrow lifted in her direction and shortly leveled out to its former line. "Well, he certainly does have the ability to upset you, doesn't he?" Reversing his wheelchair from the table, he swung it toward the hall door. "I'm going to finish reading the newspaper in the other room."

Mara stared after him. She had not lost an argument with her father since he had come back after the accident. He had always given in to her. But on this issue of Sin Buchanan, he had stood his ground and gone against her wishes. Mara was fully aware that he could be as stubborn as she was.

CHAPTER FOUR

ON MONDAY MORNING Mara arrived at the cottage to find all three rooms neat and orderly. There were no dirty dishes in the sink or an unmade bed. No magazines or papers were scattered around the living room. A list of grocery items was taped to the refrigerator door for Mara to obtain for the following weekend. It took less than an hour for her to dust and sweep the cottage.

During the week, she interviewed three women who responded to the advertisement she had placed in the paper. Two of them did not have transport and the third had simply not impressed her. So on Friday she was the one who bought the groceries and aired the cottage in preparation for Sin's arrival, finishing well before noon to avoid accidentally meeting him.

On Saturday and Sunday mornings, Mara saw him out jogging. Both times she was washing the breakfast dishes. Each time he lifted a hand in a casual wave in the direction of the window above the sink, but neither time did he approach the house. Mara didn't wave back, and she didn't care if the omission was rude. She didn't mention to her father that she had seen him nor that Sin had waved to her.

When she went to the cottage on the next Monday

morning to clean, she discovered some changes had
been made over the weekend. An old-fashioned
davenport with upright armrests was positioned in
front of the fireplace. It was upholstered in a plush
fabric patterned with varying shades of green. An
alpaca area rug in its natural cream color covered the
square of floor between the davenport and fireplace.

An old easy chair in a deep shade of gold sat to one
side. A tall floor lamp with a forest green shade stood
beside it along with a combination table and maga-
zine rack of carved oak. A rolltop desk was against
one wall with its matching straight-backed chair. The
bareness of the walls was alleviated by framed prints
of countryside scenes done by local artists.

A few touches were still needed, but this beginning
was pleasing. Yet Mara found herself wondering
somewhat critically how much of the decor was due
to the redhead's influence rather than to Sin
Buchanan's taste.

The cleaning that needed to be done was less than
before. There was a basket of dirty sheets and towels
in the utility room. Mara washed and dried them. As
she started to put them away, she checked first to be
certain clean sheets had been put on the bed and that
it hadn't been made up without them.

It hadn't. A pair of chocolate satin sheets were on
the bed. They felt smooth and sexy to the touch. A
fitting choice for a bachelor's bed, Mara thought, a
curious rage building within her.

Quickly she finished putting the clean laundry
away and returned to her own home. She didn't mention to her father the changes that had been made at

the cottage. They had both avoided any topic connected with Sin Buchanan since their discussion more than a week ago.

As she started to get lunch ready, the telephone rang. Mara didn't pay any attention to its demanding ring, knowing her father would answer it in the other room.

"It's for you, Mara," he called to her.

"I'm in the middle of getting lunch. Tell whoever it is that I'll call back later." She continued peeling the shells off the hard-boiled eggs.

"It's long distance," said Adam.

"Long distance?" she echoed, and rinsed her hands under the running tap. "I'll be right there!"

She hurried toward the study while drying her hands on a towel. A frown creased her forehead as she mentally ran through the possible identity of her long-distance caller. Adam was behind the large desk when she entered, and he handed her the telephone receiver. She missed the bright light gleaming in his eyes.

"This is Mara Prentiss."

"Thank you, Miss Prentiss. One moment, please," the impersonal voice of the operator responded, and she directed her next words to the person on the other end of the line. "I have your party for you now, sir."

"Thank you, operator. Miss Prentiss? This is Sin Buchanan." His familiar voice sounded so close that Mara wouldn't have been surprised to discover he was in the next room. Every inch of her seemed to become suddenly very alert. "How are you?"

The polite phrase prompted a polite response. "Fine, thank you." Mara had taken it as an impersonal, automatic inquiry. She glanced at her father and realized he had known all along who was calling. She turned her back to him.

"Then your arm is all right?" It was a questioning statement.

"My arm?" Mara frowned at the telephone.

"Yes, I thought it might be broken. Usually when you wave at a person, they wave back unless there's something wrong." The comment was offered in a disinterested fashion as if Sin didn't really care to hear any explanation of why she hadn't had the courtesy to return his greeting.

"Oh." Mara didn't attempt an explanation. "Was that why you called?"

"Yes, as well as to learn how you're progressing with my housekeeper," he told her.

That was the primary reason for the phone call, Mara knew. The previous remark had just been made to needle her. "I've interviewed three women so far. Would you like me to send you their applications and references?"

"Did you consider any of the three suitable for the position?" Sin countered.

"No." She kept her voice coolly restrained and forced her fingers to relax the strangling grip they had on the receiver.

"Then there isn't any reason for me to look at the applications, is there, Miss Prentiss?" There was an indulgent ring to his voice as if he were reasoning with a child.

Mara gritted her teeth and tried not to snap at him. "No, I suppose not."

"Please keep me informed." It was closer to an order than a request.

"I will," she promised with cool dignity.

"Goodbye, Miss Prentiss."

"Goodbye," Mara responded, and replaced the receiver on its cradle without waiting to hear if he had anything further to add.

"That was Sin Buchanan, wasn't it?" her father asked.

"Yes," she admitted. "He just called to see if I'd found someone to clean the cottage for him."

"What was that about your arm?" He eyed the taut line of her mouth thoughtfully.

"Somewhere he got the mistaken impression that I'd injured it." Mara shrugged with feigned ignorance of the cause.

"Where did he get that idea?" Adam questioned.

"I really don't know," she lied. "You'll have to excuse me, I have some soup warming on the stove."

That week Mara interviewed two more applicants for the position. Neither of them did she hire on Sin's behalf. When the second had left following the interview, Adam rolled his wheelchair out of the study.

"That woman sounded capable. Why didn't you hire her?" he asked.

"She sounded capable," Mara agreed, stressing the verb as qualification. "But her hair wasn't combed, her blouse needed ironing, and she had dirt under her fingernails."

"So?"

"If she's that careless with her appearance, what makes you think she'd take any more pains to keep the cottage neat and tidy?" she retorted.

"You could be right," Adam conceded. "But keep in mind, Mara, that no one is going to be as perfect as you are."

There was a painful throbbing in her temples. Mara rubbed a forefinger against it and sighed. "Why don't you just be quiet, Adam?" It carried the faintest sound of a defeated plea for peace. She let her hand fall to her side and lifted her head, giving herself a mental shake. "Did you have those notes ready for me to type?"

"Yes, they're on the desk," he replied, and watched her closely as she walked from the living room.

ANOTHER WEEKEND came and went. The only glimpse Mara had of her tenant was when he went for his morning jog. He always looked in the direction of the kitchen window, but he no longer waved.

On Monday morning Mara found a few more additions to the cottage. A wooden bookshelf was against one wall of the living room, complete with a varied selection of books. An antique mantel clock was above the fireplace, flanked by a pair of hurricane lamps. Some clothes were left in the bedroom closet and chest of drawers. All were masculine, a fact Mara couldn't help noticing. The expected list of supplies was taped to the refrigerator. The careless scrawl of Sin's handwriting was becoming very familiar.

It rained most of the week. The weather remained damp and cold. The trees lost their autumn luster, their leaves turning brown and carpeting the ground. So few leaves remained on the branches that the trees looked moth-eaten and tattered.

When the sun burst through on Saturday morning, Mara took advantage of the break in the weather to rake the ankle-deep leaves from the yard. Since they were so sodden with moisture, it was hard, physical work, but it felt good to be outside after so many days of being shut in by the rain.

This sentiment was shared by her father. His wheelchair was positioned on the patio where a stream of sunlight laid a golden square on the bricks. Despite the sunshine, there was the chill of coming winter in the air. A red plaid blanket was draped across Adam's paralyzed legs to provide the warmth his fleece-lined jacket couldn't.

Mara paused to catch her breath and glanced at him. All the raking had kept her warm, but after being outside for more than an hour, she guessed he was feeling the cold.

"Don't you think it's time you went inside, Adam?" She leaned the rake against the trunk of a tree.

"Not yet," Adam refused. "This may be the last day of good weather before winter sets in. I want to enjoy every minute of it."

"Don't blame me if you freeze and catch pneumonia," Mara warned.

"I wouldn't dream of it." He smiled lazily, his handsome dark features looking years younger.

Mara shook out a large plastic garbage bag and began scooping up the leaves from the pile to stuff them inside it. The red knit of her cap made a vibrant contrast to the sable black of her hair. It provided the one spot of color in the drabness of her work clothes, the dark blue of her denims and khaki brown of her old jacket.

As she picked up the last armful of leaves, she heard her father say, "Hello, Sin. Beautiful day, isn't it?"

"It certainly is. How are you, Adam?" was his response.

In a swift glance over her shoulder she saw the tall, well-muscled man strolling toward her father. Instead of the jogging suit, he was dressed in dark blue corduroys and a fleece-lined jacket that was unbuttoned to reveal the heavy ribbing of a pale blue turtleneck sweater.

He seemed impervious to the chill in the air as he combed his fingers through the rumpled thickness of his iron-gray hair. As if feeling the quiet inspection of her gaze, Sin glanced at her.

"You're working hard, I see," he commented.

"Yes, I am." Immediately she set to work jamming the leaves into the sack already more than half-full.

"Have you had any luck finding a housekeeper?" Sin inquired.

"Not yet." Her answer was needlessly clipped and abrupt. She tried to cover it by picking up the leaves that had scattered over the edge of the bag.

"Mara is something of a perfectionist," Adam

explained in an uncomplimentary tone. "She keeps looking for the same quality in others and refuses to compromise."

Tight-lipped, Mara offered no defense since she felt she needed none. Gathering up the open end of the leaf bag, she attempted to carry it to the driveway, but the moisture of the wet leaves made it too heavy for her to lift.

"Let me carry that for you," Sin offered, and took a step toward her.

"I can handle it," she insisted with a stubborn flash of independence.

Sin hesitated, then lifted a shoulder in silent concession. Straining, Mara dragged the plastic bag across the ground. The muscles in her arms were trembling from the effort by the time she reached the driveway. Determined not to show the effect, she walked back to pick up the rake again and set to work on the leaves in the other quarter of the yard.

All the while, Sin stood near her father, talking to him and watching her. It was a distinctly unsettling experience. The last pile of leaves didn't have to be bagged since she used them to cover the flower bed in front of the house.

"Why don't you rest for a while, Mara?" her father suggested when she had finished that. "You're making me tired just watching you work. You can rake the rest of the yard tomorrow."

"I think I *will* wait until tomorrow," she agreed, taking off her work gloves and unconsciously flexing her fingers. "The forecast was for more sunshine." In truth, she was exhausted and needed a rest, if only until the afternoon. "It's getting too cold out here for you."

"You're probably right," he agreed, which told her he was getting chilled. She walked to the back of his wheelchair and turned it toward the house. So far, she had pointedly ignored the man with her father, but Adam wasn't going to follow suit. "If you aren't doing anything special, Sin, why don't you come into the house?"

Mara froze in cold anger. "I doubt that Mr. Buchanan would want to neglect... Miss Taylor for long, Adam. You overlooked the fact that she's probably waiting for him at the cottage."

"No, she isn't," Sin offered quietly. Unwillingly her dark gaze was drawn to him. "Celene didn't accompany me this weekend."

The information caught her by surprise. It unnerved her and she sought to cover her confusion by responding sharply, "What do you do? Devote one weekend a month totally to rest?"

"Something like that," he agreed lazily.

"If no one is waiting for you, is there any reason you can't come in for a while?" Adam questioned.

"None that I know of," Sin answered, his gaze flickering to Mara in silent challenge, but she refused to rise to the bait. It was one thing to argue with her father and another to argue with Sinclair Buchanan.

Without waiting for any more to be said, Mara began pushing her father's wheelchair toward the ramp leading to the front door of the house. The uneven brick walkway made the going difficult. Her arms were already tired from all the raking. When she reached the ramp, a hand came around her to grip the chair handles.

"I'll take it from here," Sin told her.

"I can manage," Mara returned stiffly.

"Your father isn't a bag of leaves, and you had enough trouble with that." He firmly pushed her out of the way and guided the wheelchair up the ramp with an ease that Mara knew she wouldn't have been able to fake.

At his backward glance to see if she was coming, Mara offered a grudging, "Thank you," and walked up the ramp to open the door. Once inside, she immediately excused herself. "I have to clean up."

Her bedroom and bath was on the second floor. As she climbed the front stairs, Sin and her father went into the study. After bathing, Mara put on a pair of camel tan slacks and a matching sweater with black and tan horizontal stripes. She used the rear staircase that opened into the kitchen. From the front of the house she could hear the muffled sound of male voices in conversation.

The coffeepot was empty, so she made a fresh pot. While the coffee perked, she put away the breakfast dishes she had left to dry on the draining board. When the coffee was finished, she poured herself a cup and sat down at the table. After the bath and change of clothes, a cup of coffee was all she needed to relax.

The door to the kitchen swung open before she had taken her first sip. The tension that she had fought so hard to remove threaded back through her nerves as Sin Buchanan walked into the room.

Minus the bulky jacket, his physique was still formidable. Even the rough weave of his sweater seemed in keeping with the raw vigor of his manliness. He paused inside the doorway, his gaze sweeping slowly over her. Mara felt his inspection as surely as if he had touched her.

"Was there something you wanted?" She was sitting rigidly in her chair, a charged alertness in her senses.

"Your father sent me in to ask if there was any coffee," Sin explained his presence in the kitchen, moving forward with a quietness that was surprising in a man his size.

The steaming cup of coffee on the table couldn't be overlooked any more than the aroma of fresh-perked coffee in the air. Mara found his level gaze difficult to meet. To avoid it, she rose from the table.

"Yes, there's coffee. I'll fix a tray and bring it in to you," she offered in a coolly unresponsive voice.

"There's no need for you to bring it in. I'll wait and carry it in myself." He came to the counter where Mara had placed a serving tray.

"It isn't necessary." She didn't want him waiting. She wanted him gone.

"Why should I walk back empty-handed?" Sin countered with infuriating logic.

Mara didn't pursue the argument as she began arranging the mugs on the tray. "I hope Adam hasn't bored you with a lot of talk about the Civil War."

She made the barbed comment for want of something to fill the silence. Her father rarely bored anyone; he had been born with the gift of charm.

Even her mother had gone on loving him after he had deserted her for another woman. Mara suspected the only reason she was immune to him was that she was his daughter.

"I don't remember his mentioning anything about the Civil War," Sin remarked. When she set the sugar bowl and spoon on the tray, he reminded her, "I don't need any cream or sugar for my coffee, thank you."

"What have you found to talk about?" Mara reached into the cupboard for the insulated coffee server.

"Many things," was his ambiguous answer.

"Including me, I suppose." There was a bitter taste in her mouth as she said that.

Sin watched silently for a moment as she poured the hot coffee from the pot into the server. "What makes you think we would have discussed you?"

"Nothing. Forget I said it," Mara shrugged, angry with herself. She set the server on the tray. When Sin would have picked it up, she stopped him. "Just a minute. I'll put some cookies on a plate." Her father knew she had baked oatmeal raisin cookies yesterday and she suspected he would send Sin back to the kitchen if she didn't include some on the tray. But in defense of her action, she explained, "Adam has a sweet tooth."

"Why do you refer to your father by his given name?" The gray head was tipped at an inquiring angle, smoke-blue eyes studying her with disconcerting directness, "In almost every other respect, you seem typically old-fashioned."

"It's what I prefer to call him," was as much as Mara would say.

"And your reasons are private," he concluded.

"My reasons are between Adam and myself. That doesn't include outsiders." Her cool glance let him know exactly to which category he belonged.

"But it has something to do with the estrangement between the two of you." He watched her arrange the cookies on a plate. "Adam mentioned he was crippled in a car accident."

"Yes, that's right." Mara replaced the lid on the cookie jar.

"It's a pity that it had to happen to such a vital man," Sin commented.

"It's possible that he got what he deserved," she suggested, knowing how callous her comment sounded and not caring. And she didn't particularly care what he thought of her for saying it.

His gaze narrowed slightly. "Do you resent so much having to take care of him?"

"I don't *have* to take care of him, Mr. Buchanan. I chose to take care of him because he's the man who fathered me." There was a haughty air to the tilt of her chin.

"It would be perfectly natural for a young single woman to resent the demands on her free time to care for her crippled father, especially a young woman as beautiful as you," he commented.

"Compliments don't mean anything to me, Mr. Buchanan." She added the plate of cookies to the tray. "I've been around Adam too long not to have learned that they have little value beyond the moment they are spoken."

"You don't care much for your father, do you, Miss Prentiss?" It was a quiet accusation.

"Do you?" she returned.

"I haven't known him very long, but he strikes me as a likable, intelligent man," he stated.

"But you don't know him as well as I do," Mara replied, indicating that this was the only explanation she needed to give.

"Mara the bitter. You were appropriately named, weren't you?" he commented.

"Weren't you?" Mara suggested smoothly.

Laughter rolled from his throat in a low chuckle. "And I thought you were the type that turned the other cheek."

"We all make mistakes, Mr. Buchanan," she murmured.

The sounds of laughter faded, but it still glinted in his eyes. "Except you, Miss Prentiss?" An eyebrow lifted in mocking question.

Determined not to let the discussion continue any further, Mara picked up the coffee tray and turned to him. "I believe you said you would carry this into the study."

The full force of his gaze was directed at her. "Is the conversation becoming too much for you?" Sin guessed accurately.

"I'm tired of being a source of amusement for you." She didn't mince words in her answer, letting them be as cold and harsh as her anger.

"You take yourself and life too seriously," he chided. "You have to learn to laugh at things."

"There are too many things that I don't find very funny, Mr. Buchanan." Again, she offered him the tray. "If you aren't going to carry this in I will."

Sin held her challenging look an instant longer before reaching for the tray. His tanned fingers naturally encountered hers as he took the tray handles from her grip. Their contact was hard and warm and brief. It seemed to leave an invisible imprint on her skin, because the sensation remained long after the contact was broken.

Alone again in the kitchen, Mara discovered her cup of coffee had become cold. She emptied it in the sink and refilled it from the pot. But she couldn't find the same contentment that had preceded Sin's entrance to the kitchen.

The house was too confining, made smaller by the voices of the two men in the study. The bright sunlight shining outside became more inviting. Mara would have preferred slipping out the back door, but her strong sense of duty wouldn't permit her to go for a walk without informing her father of her intention.

Taking her heavy plaid parka from its hook, she put it on and walked through the house to the parlor-turned-study. Sin was the first to see her when she appeared in the double doorway, but she avoided looking at him to direct her attention to Adam.

"I wanted you to know I'm going for a walk. I'll be back in an hour," she told him. "Would you like anything before I leave? More coffee?"

"Maybe some more cookies?" Adam suggested with a bright gleam in his eye. "Sin sampled them. They were very good, as usual."

"The cookies were good," Sin reaffirmed her father's statement.

"If you'd like more, I'll get them, but I wouldn't want you to spoil your lunch, Adam," said Mara.

"No, you're right. If I eat any more, I won't want lunch," he agreed, and glanced at Sin. "Mara's speciality is really lemon pie. It's always as cool and tart as its maker."

Mara turned away. "I'll be back in an hour." She walked to the front door, never hearing Sin's response to her father's jibe.

CHAPTER FIVE

THE MIDDLE OF NOVÉMBER arrived with blustering winds and cold temperatures. The ground was hard beneath Mara's feet as she trudged along the rutted track to the cottage, a small bag of groceries under her arm. It would have been faster and easier to take the car to deliver the supplies, but they were so few to carry that she had chosen to walk.

The air was sharp and clear, an invigorating morning punctuated by the puffy clouds of her breath. A swirling wind rustled the thick carpet of leaves in the woods, the dark, skeletal outlines of the tree limbs etched against the blue of the sky.

This last week Mara had rarely ventured out of the house. Adam had caught a cold and she had spent most of her time looking after him. Her life had been very sedentary and the exercise of this brisk walk felt good.

Adam's fever had broken in the night. His temperature had dropped to near normal that morning. When she had left the house, he had been resting comfortably, assuring her that he would probably sleep for an hour or so.

Glancing ahead of her, Mara saw the cedar shakes of the cottage roof through the dark columns of tree trunks. She wondered which day Sin would be coming to the house to visit her father. Since that first social visit, Sin had regularly called at the house once a weekend to see Adam. Mara had no idea what the two men talked about, and she never asked.

Nor did she revoice her objections to having Sin Buchanan as a visitor in the house. It would have given him too much importance to make an issue of his visits with her father. So Mara spent most of her time ignoring his presence in the house during his visits.

As she approached the front door of the cottage, she reached into her jacket pocket for the key. Although she had continued to run the advertisement for a housekeeper in the paper, she hadn't had any more replies. Spending a couple of hours there Monday and Friday mornings had become part of her routine, another one of the chores she did on a regular basis.

It required both hands to unlock and open the door. Setting the grocery bag on the stoop, she inserted the key in the lock and turned the doorknob at the same time as the key. She pushed the door open, slipped the key back in her pocket and picked up the groceries.

Entering the cottage, she walked across the living room to turn up the thermostat, only to discover it hadn't been turned down. She stared at it for a puzzled instant, then shrugged. Monday morning was when Adam had woken up with the chill and a fever. In her haste to get back to him, she had probably forgotten to turn the heat down in the cottage after she had cleaned.

She carried the grocery bag into the small kitchen and set it on the counter. Unbuttoning the cumbersome parka, she slipped it off and draped it on the back of a kitchen chair. The nippy walk to the cottage had numbed her senses. She had taken the first item out of the bag before she noticed a familiar aroma in the air.

In disbelief, she glanced at the coffeepot plugged into the wall, the fragant smell of fresh coffee coming from its spout. At almost the same instant she heard a footstep from the vicinity of the bedroom, and pivoted toward the sound.

Sin's frame filled the archway to the bedroom. Clad only in a pair of rough brown denims, he walked into the kitchen. The hard, muscled chest looked deceptively trim. His naked skin was the color and smooth texture of leather stretched across his build, broken only by the V-shaped pattern of golden dark chest hairs.

The frosted steel hair was uncombed, its thickness in attractive disarray. Lines of sleep had softened the harsh carving of his features, but his eyes were alert as he took in the look of shock on Mara's face.

"Good morning." His greeting sounded so natural that it made her wonder if she had got her days mixed up. Was it Friday or Saturday? No, it definitely was Friday.

"What are you doing here?" She recovered enough to demand, then remembered, "I didn't see your car outside."

"You didn't look. My car is there, parked along-side of the cottage," Sin informed her, his steel-blue eyes regarding her with lazy interest.

Alongside the cottage—that explained it, Mara realized. Since she had walked instead of driving, her angle of approach to the cottage hadn't given her a glimpse of the far side where his car was.

"Then you're the one who turned the thermostat up and made coffee," she concluded, relieved that it hadn't been an oversight on her part.

"I must be," he agreed, "unless there's a ghost haunting the cottage that you didn't tell me about." His mouth curved into a half grin. "Did you think you were going mad?"

"I...I had a lot of things on my mind," Mara faltered in her own defense. "Adam has been sick with a cold all week. He's better now. But it was possible I might have overlooked a few things Monday."

"Not you," he taunted. "You're Miss Perfect."

"Why are you here?" His biting comment brought a chill to her voice. "It isn't Saturday."

"I decided at the last minute to come up a day early. Is that all right?" Sin asked, knowing that he didn't require her permission. "I don't recall reading any restriction in the lease that said I didn't have the use of the cottage seven days a week."

"Of course there wasn't," Mara retorted impatiently. "But you could have let me know you were changing your routine."

"I told you it was a last-minute decision. I didn't think you would appreciate a telephone call in the middle of the night." His explanation held a hint of challenge.

"The middle of the night," she unconsciously repeated his phrase.

"Yes, it was after midnight before I decided to drive up here a day early," Sin elaborated on his previous explanation.

At that hour of the night, Mara doubted that he was alone. That thought prompted another that maybe he hadn't made the journey alone. She glanced beyond Sin to the bedroom where a corner of the sleep rumpled brown satin sheets could be seen.

Sin followed the direction of her look and her thoughts. "There's no one with me, if that's what you're wondering." Amusement edged the hard corners of his mouth when her dark gaze flew back to him.

"You've been spending more and more of your weekends alone lately," Mara observed. "Aren't you worried that you might get bored without anyone to entertain you?"

"It's possible," he conceded dryly. "But if it gets too dull around here, I have the consolation of being able to sharpen my wits with you."

Why had she ever got involved in a conversation with him in the first place, Mara wondered angrily. He took malicious delight in laughing at her, finding something to poke cynical fun at no matter what she said or did. She turned away and began taking out her displeasure at the situation on the items in the grocery bag.

"I've had a long week, Mr. Buchanan. I'm too

tired from taking care of Adam to engage in a battle of words with you," she issued tightly.

His astute gaze investigated her profile, noticing the strain etched in her features but unable to guess that he was the cause of most of it. Her eyes were large black smudges against the ivory cream of her complexion. The line of her finely drawn mouth was tense, her expression rigidly contained to be without emotion.

Sin walked to where the coffeepot was plugged in only a few feet from her. Opening the cupboard door above it, he took out two cups and set them on the counter.

"Why don't you take a break for a few minutes, Mara, and have a cup of coffee with me?" he suggested. "It's fresh and hot. The groceries can wait until later."

Resentment smoldered that he should suddenly begin using her given name and pretend a solicitous concern for her well-being. She flashed him an icy look as he filled the first cup with hot coffee.

"I have no desire to have coffee with you!" The sharpness of her retort flung his invitation back in his face.

The pot was set back on the counter as a heavy silence filled the air, charging the atmosphere. His steady blue gaze was on her, piercing the cool.

"Is it that you have no desire to have coffee with me. . . or simply that you have no desire?" His question was a low, accusing challenge.

Mara hesitated only an instant before answering

coldly, "Both." She continued unpacking the bag
her movements as brisk and rapid as she could make
them without throwing things around.

"You shouldn't say things like that." Sin's voice
changed subtly, an undefinable quality entering its
low pitch. "It challenges a man to prove you're a
liar."

"Which says something about the arrogance of
men, doesn't it?" Mara countered with contempt.

"Or the trait of a woman to be provocative," he
suggested smoothly.

"I wasn't lying when I said that." A loaf of bread
was in her hand, and she paused before putting it
away to turn and confront him. "And I wasn't trying
to be provocative."

"Weren't you?" Sin was closer to her than she had
realized. She started to take a breath to make a
scathing reply to his taunt when his hand touched her
neck.

His fingers began tracing the base of her throat,
exploring its hollow, and all her muscles constricted.
Mara could neither breathe in nor breathe out. Her
heartbeat was erratic, speeding up, then slowing
down as his fingertips lingered or moved over her
sensitive skin. Her gaze was locked with his and she
had the sensation of being drawn into the murky blue
depths of his eyes.

"I'll bet ice cream doesn't melt in your mouth,"
Sin declared in a soft, taunting voice that somehow
managed to caress.

The straight line of his mouth never varied. There
wasn't a hint of a curve nor a smile. He seemed oddly

detached, as if conducting some simple exercise that didn't require his concentration. His fingers began outlining the neckline of her madras blouse. At the point, they partially entered the shadowed valley of her breasts before encountering a button. Then they started their upward slant to the base of her throat.

"It doesn't melt." Her voice was choked to a husky level by the confusion of her senses. "I have to chew it up like food."

A crazy wild shaking started in her knees. No matter how she tried, she couldn't make it stop. Not as long as he was touching her, she realized. Initially she had submitted to the caress of his fingers to prove it didn't affect her. Now that she knew better, she had to bring this sudden intimacy to a close.

Fighting the threatening sensation of weakness, Mara reached up and pushed his hand from her neck. Immediately she took a step away and turned her back to him. The grip of her fingers had made indentations in the fresh loaf of bread she held.

"What's the matter?" Sin asked in a voice that said he knew.

"Nothing's the matter." Mara opened a cupboard door to put the bread away. She seemed to lack coordination. Her movements were jerky and out of time. "I'm simply not interested in sex for the sake of sex."

"Oh?" There was a curious, lazy lilt to the sound, a laid-back sort of quality. "When are you interested in sex?"

Instead of attacking him, her remark had tripped

herself. It was a question she couldn't answer and she knew she didn't dare try.

"You've had too many celibate weekends recently," she told him. "Call Celene and have her visit you; then your ego can get fed on all her 'Sin, darlings.'"

He tipped back his head, amused laughter rolling from his throat at her sniping words. "That becomes old quickly, but I never find things growing dull with you. Each time I think I have you trapped in a corner, you come charging at me from another direction."

"I don't happen to be doing it for your amusement," she snapped.

"I'm aware of that." A trace of a smile lingered, but his look was totally serious. "It's a case of self-preservation. You don't want anybody getting too close."

"If you've got the message, why don't you leave me alone?" Mara challenged coldly.

But Sin completely ignored that. "You don't want anyone to be even physically close to you. You're a young, beautiful woman, a human being. That's a statement, not a compliment," he added. "Your body was designed with procreation as the plan. Having sex doesn't necessarily go hand in hand with love. So how do you suppress your biological urges?"

"I don't see that it's any of your business." With curtness, Mara tried to elude the topic that made her feel so uncomfortable.

Pushing the cupboard door shut on the bread, she reached into the bag for a new can of coffee. But when she lifted it out, Sin took it from her hand and set it on the counter, shoving it out of her reach.

"But I want to know," he persisted.

An arm braced against the counter prevented her from reaching the coffee can. When she attempted to ignore him and turn back to the rest of the grocery items in the bag, his other arm blocked her way.

"How do you ignore the restless yearnings for an unknown something?" he questioned.

To brace his hands against the counter, Sin was forced to bend slightly. The result was to bring his gaze eye level with hers. It seemed to probe and bore deep within her to seek out the answer she couldn't voice. There was almost more than a foot of space between them, but the width seemed much smaller. Mara pressed herself more closely against the counter until its edge was digging into the small of her back.

"What do you do about the aching hollow feeling that can gnaw at your insides?" There was less demand in his question. "Or the way your body throbs to hold someone close? Don't you ever long to be caressed?"

His low, murmured questions were seducing her, awakening all needs and longings that she usually kept smothered. They were all surfacing with a new intensity. She hoped desperately that her mask of poise was in place and that this wonderful bewilderment was well hidden from him.

"And your lips—" his gaze sought their curve and a fluttering weakness started in her stomach and began to spread "—haven't they ever imagined the pressure of another mouth on them?"

Mara shook her head in denial not of his question but of the wants it was causing. Her sleek short hair gleamed blue black in the artificial light of the kitchen, its waving style sophisticated and becoming.

"Only a saint wouldn't be expected to know the craving to have someone run his fingers through your hair," Sin murmured as he, too, became entrapped in the sensuous spell of his questions. His eyes were half-closed, a glow burning its way out of their depths.

"I am a saint," Mara whispered out of desperation. "Adam will tell you that."

"No." Sin didn't believe her. "You're flesh and blood...the same way I am, but with a delightful difference."

He leaned closer, his head tipping naturally to one side as his mouth sought the curve of her lips. Her lashes swept closed, but they didn't shut out the image of him from her mind or lessen the potent virility that was his trademark.

The kiss began as a slow yet bold exploration of new territory. Gradually it began to demand more than passivity from Mara. She was to be a participant, not merely a recipient. After a tentative beginning she began to warm to the role. No longer was she pressing herself against the counter. All that space between them seemed unnecessary.

Her fingers trembled uncertainly against his bare chest until they began to enjoy the feel of his smooth, muscled flesh. The pressure of his mouth increased. The exploration was over and Sin was claiming the territory.

His hand curved itself across her back to draw her inside the circle of his arms. Mara felt the hard outline of his body pressed against hers, the heat from it burning through her clothes to her skin. Sin was no longer leaning forward, but standing at his full height. Her head was forced to tilt backward to receive his kiss.

She had the dizzying sensation that she was teetering on the brink of a discovery. She only had to let go to find out what it was. But she couldn't. With a moaning cry of regret and relief, she broke off the kiss and strained to be free of his embrace. Sin resisted her attempts for a fleeting second, then let her go.

Stepping away from him, she covered her mouth with her hand as if hiding the very nearly devastating effect of his kiss. Her breathing was rapid and shallow. She struggled to make it normal and quiet her pounding heart. Partially succeeding, she took her hand away from her face and lifted her chin in a defensive denial that anything had changed. To reaffirm it, she began unpacking the groceries again and putting them away. Sin watched her but she pretended she wasn't aware of it.

"What happened, Mara?" Sin asked quietly.

She presumed he was referring to the kiss and the suddenness with which she ended it. "Nothing happened," she denied with feigned aloofness.

"I don't buy that," he replied in a hard, decisive voice. "It had to take years to get all your feelings and emotions frozen that solidly. So what happened?

Were you jilted? Did some guy leave you standing on the church steps?''

"No, to both questions." The coffee was put away and Mara began emptying the carton of eggs into the egg rack in the refrigerator.

"Did you take a lover, then discover he was married?" he persisted.

"No." Her control was fraying. "And if any of the answers were yes, I still would have told you no because it's none of your business!"

A muscle worked along his jaw as they confronted each other. "Is your father well enough to have visitors?"

The unexpected change of subject caught Mara by surprise. It took her a moment to make the adjustment before she could answer.

"Yes, I think so."

"Good," he nodded, and raked his fingers through his gray hair as if realizing for the first time it wasn't combed. "I'll finish getting dressed and walk back with you."

"What about your coffee?" It was the first protest that came to mind. "There's a full pot here."

"Unplug it, I've had all the stimulation I want for one morning without adding caffeine." His mouth quirked at the deliberately suggestive reminder of the kiss.

"It's cold outside. You'd be better off driving," Mara tried another tactic.

"I'm getting used to the chill in the air up here."

"Really? So has Adam," she informed him with a cool look. "He says it's a case of becoming acclimatized to the perpetual draft of cold air whenever I'm around."

"Your father and I share something in common, then, don't we?" Sin gave her a sardonic glance and turned away.

As he disappeared into the bedroom, Mara called after him, "If you aren't ready by the time I'm finished here, I'm leaving without you."

There was no response to her warning and she hurried to make it come true. She had her coat on and was halfway to the front door when Sin joined her.

"I told you I wouldn't wait for you," she reminded him. Before he could accuse her of fleeing, she added in defense. "I left Adam alone in the house. I don't want to be away any longer than necessary."

"That's understandable." His hooded look seemed willing to give her the benefit of doubt.

When Sin opened the front door, Mara was careful not to accidentally brush against him as she went by. The slight flare of his nostrils indicated that he had noticed her caution. He stopped to lock the door behind them and Mara started toward the back trail.

"Not so fast!" Sin called, a thread of impatience in his voice.

"I told you I wasn't going to wait." She didn't check her stride.

After she had taken two more steps, a hand clamped down on her elbow, the thick padding of her parka sleeve lessening its tight grip, and she was hauled around to face him. Her attempt to twist away was thwarted by the hand that seized her other arm. Mara wasn't going to stoop to the indignity of struggling against his superior strength. She stood silently in his hold, glaring up at him.

His features had become hardened with anger, his eyes metallic chips of cold steel. Her heavy parka didn't lessen the impression the unyielding muscles of his thighs were making against hers, nor insulate her from the warmth of his body heat.

"What's the matter with you, Mara?" Sin demanded, his tone harsh and impatient. "I assure you I have no intention of dragging you off in the woods somewhere and raping you, if that's what's frightening you."

"Truthfully, it never occurred to me that you might be that desperate!" she spat out.

He seemed to release much of his anger in an impatiently sighed breath. "Then why do I get the feeling you're running from me?" He released her elbow and started to slide his fingers through her sleek black hair.

Mara had not recovered sufficiently from his previous caresses to withstand another. She twisted her head away from his hand in rejection of his touch.

"Let me go and leave me alone!" The instant the demand was out, she was angry. "Damn," she swore softly. "Why do you always make me sound like some Victorian virgin?" Resentment flashed in the look she sent him.

Sin did as he was asked and took a step away from her, a certain grimness to his mouth. "I wouldn't worry. You're neither meek nor mild, two essential ingredients to be classified as belonging to the Victorian era.''

Hiding her clenched fists in the pocket of her jacket, Mara started again toward the trail. "I don't know where my place is, but it isn't under any man," she declared, fighting the shaky feeling inside her.

"Literally or figuratively, is that it?" Sin taunted.

"That's it." The flat statement seemed to echo laughingly in her ears.

Mara set a brisk pace, as if trying to escape whatever was pursuing her. Sin easily kept stride with her, his long legs capable of outdistancing her if he chose. But they walked without talking.

Entering the brick house through the rear door, Mara paused to hang up her coat on the empty hook by the door. She flicked a glance in Sin's direction that didn't quite reach his face. It stopped somewhere between the second and third button of his jacket.

"Why don't you take off your coat and hang it on the rack while I see if Adam is awake?" Her voice was stilted and brittle after the long silent walk.

"Thank you, I will."

Her peripheral vision caught his movement as he started to unbutton his coat, but she was already walking toward the swinging door that led to the rest of the house. Her father's bedroom was on the ground floor. When she entered his room, his eyes were closed. She was half-afraid he was asleep. Uncertain wheth r to wake him or let him rest, she walked to his bed.

He opened his eyes and smiled wanly. "You're back."

"Yes, how are you feeling?" Her gaze inspected his face. She thought his color had improved considerably.

"Hungry," Adam said to confirm her silent assessment.

"I'll fix you some broth. By the way, you have a visitor," she added, her lips curving into a stiff smile.

"A visitor?" he frowned. "Who—Hello, Sin." He was looking beyond her to the door. "What are you doing here? Or have I lost a day?"

"You didn't lose a day. I decided at the last minute to come up a day early," Sin explained.

"I'm glad you did. Come in and sit down—not too close, though. I don't want you catching this cold," Adam laughed in warning. He glanced at his daughter as Sin sat in a straight-backed chair near the foot of the bed. "Mara was just going to bring me a cup of broth. Would like something? Coffee? Tea?"

"No, thank you," Sin refused, and didn't even glance toward Mara as she left the room.

It was a relief to have her hands and mind occupied with fixing the broth, even if it was a simple task. Unfortunately it was too quickly accomplished. She turned off the heat under the pan and poured the broth into a mug.

Her reappearance in the bedroom brought a momentary lull in their conversation. She cranked Adam's bed up so he was seated more upright and positioned the lap table in front of him.

As she walked over to get the cup of broth from

where she had left it on a side table, Sin began speaking to her father. "I'd thought I would enlist your expert services this weekend to take me on a tour of the battlefield."

"Now, I would enjoy that," Adam replied.

"You probably would." Mara set his broth on the table in front of him. "But you can't do it this weekend."

"I feel fine." He dismissed her assertion with a positive nod.

"Mara's right." The agreement came unexpectedly from Sin. "It wouldn't be wise for you to be out, as cold as it is. There's no need to risk a relapse."

"You're outnumbered two to one, Adam." Mara adjusted the pillow behind his head to give him more support.

"I may be," Adam conceded, "but I hate to think that Sin is going to miss out on the tour. He's in the mood now. Who knows when he will be again?" he jested. "I've got the solution!" he declared, glancing from Sin to Mara with a bright gleam in his eyes. "Mara knows almost as much as I do about the Gettysburg battle. She can take you this weekend."

Holding her breath, Mara shot a quick look at Sin. Cynicism glittered in his eyes. Adam had known it was the last thing in the world she would want to do.

"It's thoughtful of you to volunteer your daughter," Sin replied. "I'm sure she probably knows a lot about the battlefield since she's assisted you in your research. But I suspect she'll be reluctant to guide me through it."

"Why?" There was too much innocence in her father's dark eyes when he looked at her. "You showed our cousin from California around the park, and a friend of mine from Atlanta."

Mara wasn't going to explain to Adam that the circumstances were different. Those other people were virtually strangers to her, whereas Sin. . . . No, she wasn't about to explain to her father.

"I wouldn't have any objections to acting as a guide for Mr. Buchanan," she lied bravely. "But I have too many things to do this weekend that I wasn't able to get done during the week. Also, I want to do some baking to get ready for Thanksgiving. I wouldn't have enough free time to do justice to the area until Monday. I'd want to wait until then anyway to be certain you've fully recovered."

"Couldn't you postpone a few of those things?" Adam argued.

"I postponed too many things while you were sick." Mara stood firm.

"That's all right," Sin offered. A light was dancing in his eyes. "Monday is fine with me. What time?"

"What time?" Mara repeated, feeling that she had just been swallowed in a trap. She glanced at her father, certain he had been part of the conspiracy, but he looked just as surprised as she was.

"Will you be here on Monday?" he asked with astonishment.

"Yes. As a matter of fact, I won't be driving back to Baltimore until the weekend after Thanksgiving," Sin told them.

"You didn't tell me anything about that at the cottage," Mara accused.

"You didn't ask me," he countered, a dark brow quirking briefly to mock her. "I intended to mention to you over coffee that you wouldn't need to come Monday to clean, but we got sidetracked with other issues. I would have remembered to tell you sooner or later," he shrugged, and Mara couldn't help wishing it had been sooner. "What time on Monday?" he repeated his earlier question.

"I don't know." Agitated, Mara couldn't find any way out of the mess. "After lunch, I suppose. That's when Adam usually rests.

"After lunch on Monday. I'll look forward to the tour." His smile held a wealth of complacency.

CHAPTER SIX

A FEW MINUTES after one o'clock on Monday, Sin's silver gray car turned into the driveway. Mara had just finished drying the last of the lunch dishes. She folded the damp towel neatly and hung it on the rack to dry. At the knock on the door, she ran a smoothing hand over her black hair and went to answer it.

When she opened the door, Sin didn't immediately enter. His gaze raked her, lingering briefly on the slimness of her bare legs beneath her dirndl skirt.

"Aren't you going to back out?" he challenged.

"No." Mostly because she wouldn't give him the satisfaction. "Excuse me." She turned away from the open door, not caring if he came in or stayed outside in the cold. "I'll tell Adam I'm leaving."

As she left the kitchen, Mara heard the door close and guessed that Sin was waiting inside. At her father's bedroom door, she knocked once and went in.

"I heard the car drive in." Adam spoke before she did. "Was it Sin?"

"Yes. I wanted to let you know I was leaving and double-check to see if there was anything you needed '' Mara told him.

"Not a thing," he assured her. "The telephone is here by the bed. So are my notes and books, and a pitcher of water."

"Are you positive you're feeling all right?" But he looked so disgustingly healthy that Mara knew there wasn't much hope.

"I'm fine." A knowing smile curved his mouth. "Sin is waiting for you. Don't you think you should be going?"

"Yes." Her hands felt moist; the nervousness she was trying so hard to conceal was surfacing. "If you need anything—"

"I have half a dozen telephone numbers to cover every kind of an emergency," he interrupted. "Have a good time, Mara."

Sheer perversity made her say, "I sincerely doubt it." She left the bedroom and retraced her steps to the kitchen. Sin was waiting near the back door. His gaze swung lazily to her when she entered. "I'm ready to leave if you are," she said briskly.

"You mean your father hasn't suffered an unexpected relapse?" He reached forward to open the door for her.

"Adam is feeling very fit." Taking her full-length winter coat, Mara draped it over her shoulders and swept past him. Angry, she was determined to remain cool in the face of his taunts.

"We'll take my car." Sin followed her outdoors.

"Since I'll be doing the driving, I would prefer mine," Mara insisted.

"Mine is already warm. I've left the motor running

to keep it that way," he said. "Besides, it's more comfortable than yours to ride in. And I'm sure you're a perfect driver no matter what car you're in."

Mara didn't want to waste her energy arguing over which car they were going to take; she would rather conserve it in case it was needed later. And she didn't want to admit she was nervous at the prospect of driving Sin's luxury model.

The car's heater had kept the interior comfortably warm. Not needing the coat, Mara stowed it in the backseat before sliding onto the plushly upholstered seat behind the wheel. She quickly studied the dashboard while Sin walked around the car to sit on the passenger side. When he was safely in and the door was shut, she backed out of the driveway onto the road. The car seemed to practically drive itself, so smoothly did it handle.

"I owe you an apology," he said after they had gone almost a mile.

"An apology?" she repeated coolly. "What for?"

"I honestly expected you to come up with some feeble excuse not to take me on this tour," he admitted, sliding her a curious glance.

"Were you hoping I'd back out because you were already growing bored with the idea of touring the battlefield?" Mara questioned, sparing a glance from the road. "Because if you've changed your mind—"

"I haven't changed my mind." Sin killed that hope.

"It was possible that you only mentioned you

wanted to go out of deference to Adam," Mara defended her previous suggestion.

"It was partly out of deference to him, and partly out of my own curiosity to see it with a knowledgeable person to explain it to me. Of course, at the time I expected that person to be Adam. It never occurred to me that you would be the one who would act as my guide," he told her.

Mara flexed her grip of the steering wheel, feeling a surge of anger rush through her. "You tricked me into this!" she accused.

"You volunteered," Sin reminded her.

"And you know precisely why I volunteered," she snapped. "Because I thought you wouldn't be here today—a vital piece of knowledge that you didn't see fit to give me."

"How was I to know it would matter?" His voice was smooth. "You sounded so sincere when you said you would be willing to show me around today." Sin paused to glance at her, but Mara continued to watch the road. "Do you want to call off the tour and go back?"

"Oh, no," she refused in a chilling tone. "You're going to have a full and complete tour of the battlefield." She was going to see that was all the satisfaction he got out of this untenable situation. "How much do you know about the events leading up to the Battle of Gettysburg?"

"Some, why don't you refresh my memory?" he suggested dryly.

"The war between the states was in its third year. The North had not won a majory victory although

General Grant had Vicksburg surrounded and under siege," Mara began. "The morale in the North was very low. The people were getting weary of war. A consensus was growing among the citizenry of the North that the South should be allowed to secede from the Union—they wanted to end the war and all the bloody fighting and killing. Aware that the North had lost heart, General Robert E. Lee turned his war-hardened veteran army north. He felt a victory on northern soil would win the Confederacy the needed support of the European countries, and perhaps even force a peace with the North, so he directed his army of seventy-five thousand here to southern Pennsylvania."

"And no one opposed him along the way?" Sin questioned.

Mara slowed the car as they entered the town of Gettysburg. "No one. The Union knew Lee was moving, but their patrols couldn't locate his army, which sounds unbelievable when you realize his supply train of wagons was forty-two miles long. Both armies knew they would have to meet, but they didn't know where. They first encountered each other west of Gettysburg, so that's where we'll start our tour."

Turning west on Chambersburg Pike, Mara stole a glance at Sin's jutting profile. It seemed sculpted in bronze, the strong, male lines emphasized. The skies outside were overcast, a gray background for the burned silver of his hair. He seemed distant, his thoughts elsewhere. Yet his vitality was a forceful thing. Even now it permeated the air surrounding

of the Confederate battle plan to encircle the Union army ended the day in a stalemate.

As she drove slowly along Confederate Avenue, it seemed fitting that the trees were stark and bare of leaves and the grass brown and yellowed with autumn. A wide, open field stretched before them to Seminary Ridge.

"Since Lee's plan to outflank the Union army failed the day before, he decided to send his army straight up the middle of their defenses, split them in two," Mara recounted. "That is the field Pickett's men had to cross—no trees, no cover. The rebel soldiers were lined up in rows, shoulder to shoulder, for a mile and a half, facing Seminary Ridge. You've heard the story of the Charge of the Light Brigade? It couldn't match Pickett's charge. They marched across this field with Northern soldiers blowing holes in them, but they didn't stop. The creeks around Gettysburg ran red with blood. Less than an hour later, ten thousand of Pickett's fifteen thousand men were casualties and they'd failed to take the ridge."

"Stop here," Sin ordered, and Mara turned off the highway to park alongside the road. "Let's get out and walk."

A cold wind whipped at her as she stepped from the car. She reached into the back for her coat and slipped it on. She didn't bother to button it, holding the front closed with her hands thrust into the pockets. Sin was standing a short distance from the car, overlooking the field Pickett's men crossed. Mara walked forward to join him.

"Lee was here waiting when the survivors came

back," Mara continued her narrative in a low voice. "Some said there were tears in his eyes when he met them. He didn't blame them for failing. He told them it was his fault because he had believed they were 'invincible.' The next day, Lee led the remnants of his Confederate army and retreated south. It was July 4, 1863."

A brief shiver quaked her shoulders, but it wasn't caused by the cold wind blowing around her ears. It was a sober understanding of why the Union soldiers felt no glory in their victory that long-ago day. It had cost too many lives on both sides.

Her sideways glance encountered Sin's gaze. The look in his eyes seemed to hold a half-formed question, and she was curious to find out what it was.

"Was there something you wanted to ask?" she inquired, keeping her tone distantly impersonal.

Sin glanced toward the battlefield as if he wasn't going to answer. He stood quietly, the collar of his coat turned up against the wind.

"I was just wondering," he spoke at last, "whether you were beginning to believe you were invincible because you've repulsed so many assaults in the past."

The surroundings and all the talk about the battle had lulled Mara's senses, but now they came to full alertness. Annoyed with herself for permitting Sin to make a personal comment, she turned toward the car.

"From here we'll drive to the national cemetery where Lincoln made his address," she told him.

The restraining touch of his hand on her arm halted Mara and her gaze lifted in cold challenge from his hand on her arm to his face. One side of his mouth curved upward in amusement. She silently cursed him for being so damned impregnable.

"You remind me of a turtle." Sin eyed her steadily. "The minute anyone approaches, you withdraw inside your armored shell." Something flickered in his look that tripped up the even rhythm of her heartbeat. "But beneath its hard exterior a turtle is very vulnerable."

Entrapped by the light in his eye, she wasn't aware of his hand moving to slide inside her coat and across her stomach. She drew a sharp breath of unwilling enjoyment as his other hand pushed its way inside her coat to spread his fingers over her skin.

Before the cold air could penetrate the opened front of her coat she was drawn against the warmth of his solid frame. Her hands came out of her pockets to grip the bulging muscles of his arms in a halfhearted attempt at resistance. His mouth covered hers with sensual perfection.

The subtle pressure of his kiss sent all repressions fleeing. At his invitation Mara responded freely, her lips parting under the provocative insistence of his. His experience was devastating to her previously unbreached defenses.

An exploding desire flamed through her nerves, her body quivering in the pleasurable aftershock. The intimate caress of his hands over her soft flesh was igniting new sensations that fevered her racing pulse.

Under his touch, her breasts seemed to swell to fit the cup of his hand.

When his mouth moved slowly across her cheek, the warmth of his breath fanned her already hot skin. Sin paused near her ear to nip sensually at the lobe, then explored the pulsing vein in her neck all the way to the sensitive hollow of her throat. The quivering weakness he evoked was delightful.

A car went by. Had there been more? In her shattered condition, Mara wasn't sure. It gradually penetrated her dazzled mind that they were standing out in the open, in plain view of anyone who drove past.

Her sense of propriety struggled with her new, wildly sweet emotions and won. Twisting her head toward her shoulder, she blocked his stirring exploration of her neck and throat. She didn't have the strength nor the will to slip out of his arms, but she was able to elude the attempt of his compelling mouth to retake possession of her lips. .

"Stop!" Her husky voice betrayed the disturbed state of her senses, a condition that didn't improve as she felt his lips moving against her silky hair. "Sin, people can see us!"

After an instant's hesitation he slowly lifted his head, his hands sliding to her waist. Mara felt the tenseness of his muscles, his reluctance communicated to her along with the sheer power of his control. She kept her face averted from his much too observant slate-blue eyes, not wanting him to see how thoroughly he had conquered her.

The awareness of his gaze and the touch of his

hands were too unnerving. She pushed at his arms, wanting to be released, but lacking the will to achieve freedom on her own. As his hold loosened, she turned away and put distance between them with a hurried step. She pulled the front of her coat together as if by doing so she could erase the invasion of his hands.

But nothing could erase the way he had aroused emotions she had intended to remain forever dormant. A spurious glance in his direction caught his calculating look. Sin was aware of it: she could read the knowledge in the provocative depths of his eyes. Never had she felt so transparent and never had she loathed the sensation more.

As she walked swiftly to the car, she stared blindly in front of her and refused to let her gaze wander to Sin. She was inside the car before she realized she had climbed in on the passenger side. Rather than admit she had been too shaken by his embrace and its aftermath to know what she was doing, she stayed where she was.

When she reached out to pull the passenger door shut, Sin's hand was there to temporarily halt hers. "Aren't you driving?" His voice was too bland for the words to be an inquiry. It was much too knowing.

Mara wouldn't look at him. "You drive." A tug of the door pulled it out of his yielding grasp.

Her hands were clenched tightly in her lap, betraying the strain she was under, as Sin walked around the car to the driver's side. After starting the motor, he paused to look at her.

"You'll have to give me directions to the cemetery. I don't know how to get there from here," he said.

Mara still wouldn't meet his gaze as she stiffly faced the front of the car. "We aren't going to the cemetery. The tour is over, so you can drive me home."

She half expected an argument or at the very least some taunting comment, but there was none forthcoming. Sin shifted the car out of parking gear and turned it onto the road. As they drove away, Mara turned her head to look out the side window at the field of Pickett's charge paralleling their route. She knew what it was like to believe yourself invincible, only to be defeated by a superior force.

The drive back seemed extraordinarily long. With each passing mile the silence grew more oppressive and the atmosphere more charged. The air seemed to crackle with the volatile undercurrents. Sin Buchanan was the epitome of everything Mara detested in the male gender, and the intensity of her dislike increased with each minute she was forced to endure his presence.

The wooded landscape became more familiar as they approached the red brick farmhouse. When it came into sight, Mara's nerves seemed to scream with relief. But Sin didn't slow the car at the driveway. Instead he continued along the graveled road.

"You've missed the driveway." Mara turned in her seat to look back at it. "Where are you going?" Her tone hovered between an accusation and a demand, desperation gnawing at her stomach.

His gaze left the road long enough to slide over her

face in quick assessment. "You seem shaken by our...tour." Deliberately he hesitated over the cause and chose the wrong reason to prove he knew the true one. "I thought we'd have some coffee at the cottage so you could have time to recover."

Mara was fully aware of what would happen at the cottage. His seduction of her would continue, this time in total privacy and before she had a chance to recover her equilibrium. Conscious as she was of the crazy upheaval the prospect was igniting within her, there was no way she was going to accompany him to the cottage.

"I thought I'd made it clear before, Mr. Buchanan, that I don't want...coffee with you. Turn the car around and take me home," she ordered in a frigid voice, iced by an admitted fear of what might happen.

"Mr. Buchanan?" He arched an amused eyebrow in her direction. "I much prefer it when you call me Sin. You had no difficulty with the name earlier."

Had she called him Sin? With hot awareness Mara realized she had, and his arrogant reminder of the fact increased her anger.

"Turn the car around, Mr. Buchanan." She stiffly reminded him that he hadn't complied with her order and addressed him formally to affirm her previous usage.

With an expressive shrug of his shoulder, Sin used the lane to the cottage to turn into and reverse the car. His manner suggested he felt there would be future opportunities to pursue his objective, namely her.

"If you want to have coffee at the house, that's all right with me," he said, slowing the car this time to turn into the driveway. "I only thought you wouldn't want Adam to see you in your present state."

"Adam has nothing to do with this. And I'm not inviting you in for coffee. Why should I?" she challenged. "I don't even like you!"

The car had stopped beside the house. As Mara turned to open her door, Sin's hand captured her chin and twisted it around so that she faced him.

"At the moment, it's yourself that you're not liking very much, not me," Sin informed her with an indolent tilt of his mouth.

Before she could jerk away, he was planting a hard, punishing kiss on her lips for lying to herself. The searing fire of his mouth was removed without her having an opportunity to resist it. That knowing light was in his eyes as he surveyed her widened look.

It goaded her into responding, "Don't ever come up to the house again unless you're invited...or it's in connection with some business about the cottage."

With the cold order issued, Mara climbed out of the car and slammed the door. Her shoulders were rigidly squared and her spine ramrod straight as she walked to the house. She didn't look back when she heard Sin backing out of the driveway. She knew his expression would be one of amusement.

Inside the house, she had barely had time to take off her coat before her father was calling, "Mara, is that you?"

Irritation rippled through her. She was not being allowed even a moment to marshal her composure. Smothering a sigh, she draped her coat over a hanger and hung it up. Adam was bound to ask about the tour and Sin, and attempting to postpone his questions would only heighten his curiosity.

"Yes, it's me, Adam," she answered, her voice raised to make herself heard.

Knowing he expected her to come to his room, she started in its direction. In front of a mirror, she paused to glance at her reflection. The slight flush to her complexion could be blamed on the cool temperature outside, but she could think of no excuse for the troubled darkness of her brown eyes or her still unsteady pulse. She hoped they were two things Adam wouldn't notice.

"You're back early, aren't you?" He frowned curiously when she appeared in the doorway to his bedroom.

"As chilly as it was outdoors, we didn't spend much time walking around. A driving tour of the battlefield doesn't take very long," she offered an explanation.

"Even driving you made record time," Adam went on. "You couldn't have taken Sin on a very comprehensive tour."

"I skipped a few places," admitted Mara, trying not to be to defensive. "He wasn't all that interested in the tour to begin with."

"Where is Sin?" Adam glanced behind her as if expecting to see him. "Didn't you invite him in for coffee?"

"Certainly not!" She snapped out the answer, her memory too fresh with Sin's invitation, supposedly for coffee.

"That wasn't very considerate." The sharpness of reprimand was in his voice.

"Why? He had his tour." And more, she could have added, because he'd had more than she had intended him to receive.

"I would have thought you'd feel a certain sense of obligation—" Adam began.

Provided with the opening, Mara attacked in order to divert the conversation. "You know nothing about obligation, Adam. That and 'duty' and 'loyalty' are three words that aren't in your vocabulary."

His handsome features hardened in anger. "No? I think I have a better understanding of their meaning than you do."

"Ha!" It was a contemptuous sound. "I suppose the way you were able to twist their meaning is what enabled you to desert mother and me."

"I never deserted either of you," he retorted harshly. "My sense of duty and obligation is what prompted me to make your future and your mother's secure from financial worries. Rosemary always came first in my loyalty and devotion because she was the mother of my child—you."

"You can't expect me to believe that," Mara hurled at him. "Your attempts to justify the way you behaved are sickening!"

"If you're sickened by anything, it should be what you've become," accused Adam.

"What *I've* become?" Mara repeated with haughty disdain.

"Yes, you with your high-and-mighty airs. You've put yourself up on some pedestal and encased yourself in marble." His brown eyes regarded her with disgust. "You have no feelings, no emotions, no heart. If you weren't my daughter, I would despise you. As it is, I can't make up my mind whether I pity you or myself."

Mara whitened under his stinging attack. "I don't need your pity," she countered.

"No, you don't need anything," Adam agreed in a colder tone than he had ever used. "And I thank God I'm not you. Because I need, and I feel, and I'm alive. But you're a bitter shadow of a woman with no substance and no value."

"How can you say such things to me?" Tears burned the back of her eyes, but she refused to let them escape.

"It hurts, Mara. Believe me, it hurts to say it." There was pain in his face. "I'd give anything if I had a daughter who would run to this bed and fling herself in my arms, a daughter who would cry and ask, 'Daddy, why did you leave me when I loved you so?' "

A tightness gripped her throat. "How would you answer that?"

"I don't know." Adam gave her a level look. "I've never had a daughter who came to me and asked that question. Only a daughter who's capable of love and emotion could ask it. If she were capable of feeling, she would probably understand my answer."

"What you mean is she'd be gullible enough to be taken in by your lies." Despite the bitterness of her answer, Mara was being torn in two. His words were appealing to the emotions Sin had aroused. She felt herself weakening. The instant the words were out, she heard herself retracting them. "I didn't mean that, Adam." Turning away from him, she managed a confused, "I don't know what I mean anymore."

As she blindly fled his bedroom, she heard his murmured, "That's a beginning."

CHAPTER SEVEN

THE CONFRONTATION had left an unexpected state of neutrality in its wake. Mara couldn't explain it. She only knew she couldn't summon her previous aloofness when she was around her father. One of the barriers she had erected had fallen down, but she hadn't discovered which one it was.

Opening the oven door, she pulled out the shelf holding the roasting pan on it and basted the turkey it contained. Its succulent flesh was a rich golden brown. An aromatic blend of sage and giblet stuffing filled the kitchen, emanating from the cavity of the bird.

Beside the roasting pan was a pan of candied sweet potatoes. Cooling on the kitchen counter was a pumpkin pie. On top of a burner on the stove, peas were simmering in a pan. The refrigerator contained a relish tray and cranberry salad. The menu for the noontime meal was that of a traditional Thanksgiving dinner.

"Mmm, something smells good," her father declared as he rolled his wheelchair into the kitchen. "How long before dinner is ready?"

"I'm just waiting on the turkey and the sweet potatoes." Mara slid the shelf into the oven and closed the door. "Another half hour or so, and they'll be done."

"When are you going to set the table?" Adam questioned.

"I have." She absently motioned to the one in the kitchen while she searched for the right size lid to fit the pan holding the peas.

"Since it's Thanksgiving, don't you think we should eat in the dining room?" he suggested. "It's a special day and a special dinner, turkey and all the trimmings."

"I suppose we could." Finding the lid, she covered the pan and turned off the heat to let the peas steam cook. "I want to put the dinner rolls in the oven first, then I'll set the table in the other room."

"You don't need to. I'll do it," Adam volunteered, and wheeled his chair to the kitchen table. "We'll need another place setting, though."

"What?" Mara frowned in confusion. Her first thought was that she had inadvertently put a dirtied plate on the table, believing it to be clean.

"There are only two settings here." Adam stacked the two plates on his lap and laid the silverware on top of them. "We need another."

"For who?" She stiffened, already guessing the answer.

"For whom?" he corrected her grammar.

"You didn't invite Sin Buchanan for dinner?" she accused. She hadn't seen Sin since Monday and she wanted to keep it that way.

"Yes, I did," said Adam as if it was the most reasonable thing in the world to do.

"Well, you can just uninvite him!" She slammed the cupboard door after taking out the sheet pan for the dinner rolls.

"Mara!" He clicked his tongue at her in teasing remonstration. "Where is my charitable daughter with the halo circling her head? It's a holdiay, a time to sit down with your fellow man and give thanks for the bountiful goodness we've been granted."

"I am not sitting at any table with him." Her angry denial lacked its usual conviction. She frowned and wondered where her vehemence had gone.

"It's Thanksgiving. Here Sin is in Pennsylvania, without any family or close friends. Would you really make him eat his holiday dinner alone?" It wasn't really a question. "There's so much turkey and food, the two of us couldn't possibly eat it all. We'll be having leftovers for a week. It isn't as if we can't spare the food."

"I never said it was," she protested.

"The Pilgrims sat down to dinner with the Indians. Surely you can sit at a table with Sin?" His whole manner was teasing as opposed to deriding.

Mara found it difficult to take offense at his attitude. "And if I can't?" She tried to challenge him with her usual coldness but her tone fell short of its mark.

"It seems to me you have two choices," her father answered. "Either you can eat in the kitchen while Sin and I have dinner in the dining room. Or else you can tell him he isn't welcome here for dinner. You'd better make up your mind, because here he is now."

His last statement was followed immediately by a

knock on the door. Adam had seen Sin's approach through the door's window. Mara pivoted sharply toward the sound.

"Why did you wait until the last minute to tell me you'd invited him?" she hissed at her father, irritated because he had done it deliberately so she wouldn't have time to think of an adequate escape. "You knew I wouldn't like it."

He merely smiled. "You'd better answer the door."

Mara flashed him an angry look as she walked to answer the second knock. In a fleeting moment of vanity, she was glad she had changed into the cranberry wool dress she was wearing. It was a fitting choice for the holiday dinner, plus it was highly complimentary to her dark coloring. The minute she realized what she was thinking, Mara pushed the thought aside. Why should she suddenly care that she looked particularly attractive?

Her heart was beating a crazy tattoo against her ribs when she opened the back door. This traitorous betrayal by her body upset her. It was reflected in the troubled darkness of her eyes.

The reaction was mild compared to the sudden acceleration of her pulse when she faced Sin and met his steel-blue eyes. He, too, had dressed for the occasion in a corduroy suit of charcoal gray, a shade that enhanced the burnished silver mane of his hair.

"I was invited to dinner today." Sin gave faint emphasis to the verb to let her know he remembered her order not to come to the house unless he had been invited.

"Yes, I know," she admitted. "Adam neglected to let me know until a few minutes ago that he'd asked you to join us for Thanksgiving dinner." Indecision warred within her as she continued to stand in the doorway, the cold November air chilling her skin.

"I see." Sin took a step backward as if in anticipation of his invitation being canceled.

His apparent willingness to accept her decision forced Mara to second her father's invitation or feel excessively churlish. "It doesn't matter. There's more than enough food for three of us. Please come in, Mr. Buchanan." She used the formal term of address to let him know the invitation did not change their relationship.

His hooded gaze gave her a considering look as he inclined his head in polite acceptance. "Thank you." After Mara had stepped out of the way, he entered the kitchen to greet her father. "Hello, Adam. How are you feeling?"

"I'm glad you could come, Sin," her father replied with a veiled twinkle in his eyes. "I'm fully recovered from my cold. My only problem now is hunger."

"A problem not helped by the appetizing aroma in the air," Sin sympathized.

It was an indirect compliment to Mara's cooking, but she pretended not to hear it. She feigned a studied concentration in arranging the dinner rolls on the sheet pan, her back turned to Sin.

"I'll need that third place setting for the table, Mara," her father reminded her. "Would you hand it to me?"

Mara felt about as comfortable as a pin cushion.

Wiping her hands on a towel, she took a plate from the cupboard and silverware from the drawer and handed them to her father.

"Never mind the glasses," Adam instructed. "We'll use the crystal goblets from the china closet in the dining room." Turning his chair, he was careful not to let the plates slip from his lap. "We have time for a glass of sherry before dinner, Sin. Or something stronger, if you like."

"Sherry is fine." Sin glanced inquiringly to Mara. "Will you join us?"

"No." Her refusal was quick, self-consciously so. "Thank you, but I'd better stay here in the kitchen where I can watch the turkey."

Neither man argued the necessity of it with her and Mara was left alone in the kitchen. Listening to their voices in the dining room, she put the dinner rolls in the oven to brown and checked the turkey once more. She pottered around, finding excuses not to join them in the other room until it was time to start carrying the dishes of food in to set on the table. Even then Mara tried to be as unobtrusive as possible, not wanting to call Sin's attention to her. When she carried the turkey in on its platter, the men were seated at the table. She started to set the turkey in front of her father to carve.

"Let Sin do it," he told her. "He's more mobile than I am."

A protest hovered on the tip of her tongue, but she knew his suggestion was practical. Reluctantly she walked over to Sin's chair. Her shoulder brushed against his as she reached in front of him to set the platter down. The contact burned along her nerve ends, searing them raw. But Sin appeared impervious to it.

For Mara, it heightened an awareness that was already too high. She found herself unable to take part in the table conversation. Any attempt by either her father or Sin to include her in it was usually met by a stilted response.

The food, for all its appetizing taste, invariably seemed to become lodged in her throat, and she was glad she had kept her portions small. Her discomfort was increased by the way her gaze kept straying to Sin's strong hands. She kept remembering how they had caressed her flesh, skillfully arousing her desire. Just thinking about it sparked a similar response.

It was a relief when her plate was sufficiently clean that she could claim her hunger was satisfied. In truth, it had ceased to exist when Sin had entered the house.

"Excuse me." She rose from her chair. "While you finish, I'll dish up the desert."

"Pumpkin pie?" Adam darted her a questioning look.

"Of course," she nodded.

"With some whipped cream to go with it, I hope," he tacked on.

"Yes, I still have to whip it, but it won't take long," Mara promised, and retreated to the relative security of the kitchen.

With an electric mixer, she whipped the cream into stiff peaks. She added sugar and vanilla and whipped it again. The swinging of the kitchen door drew her gaze. Sin walked in, carrying the dinner plates.

"Clearing away some of the dishes seemed the least I could do to show my appreciation for an excellent meal," he said to explain his action.

His appearance reduced her composure to chaos. She riveted her attention on the bowl of whipping cream and the beaters whirring in its foam.

"Thank you," Her response was brittly unnatural. "I'll bring the dessert in shortly."

"I'll help you carry it in," Sin volunteered, walking to the counter where she was working.

The pie was already sliced, individual pieces on the dessert plates. All that was left to do was add a generous spoonful of whipped cream to each piece. As Sin paused beside Mara to watch her finish beating it, her sensitive radar sounded the alarm at his closeness.

"It really isn't necessary." She tried to refuse his assistance and deny his continued presence.

"I don't mind." He dismissed her protest as nothing more than a polite gesture not to be taken seriously. "Besides, I wanted to thank you privately for asking me to have dinner with you in spite of Adam's oversight."

"It wasn't my idea to invite you." She wanted that clear. Normally she would have whipped the cream another couple of minutes, but Sin's nearness prompted her to turn off the mixer. Under the circumstances, it was sufficiently blended.

"I am aware who issued the invitation," he replied dryly. "At the time, I wondered if you were. But you could have vetoed it and you didn't. So, thank you."

"You're welcome." It was a polite phrase to end the discussion.

Trying desperately to ignore him, Mara removed the beaters from the mixer. Foamy peaks of whipped cream clung to the mixer blades. She wiped the excess from them with her forefinger, the bulk of it dropping into the bowl. Some remained on her finger.

When she started to wipe it on a towel, a hand closed around her wrist, strong fingers overlapping her slender bones. The fingertip with the whipped cream was lifted to Sin's mouth. Her heart catapulted to beat somewhere in the region of her throat as he slowly and erotically licked the whipped cream from her finger.

All the while, his gaze held hers. Mara felt herself drowning in the unfathomable depths of his blue eyes. She was being pulled down, down, with no hope of being rescued and no will to care.

"Stop it, Sin," she whispered the choked plea.

Satisfaction glinted briefly in his expression, but he didn't let go of her wrist. "Stop it, who?" He demanded that she repeat his given name.

"Sin," Mara breathed in surrender.

She was already swaying toward him when his mouth began its descent to her lips. An iron band encircled her waist to flatten her breasts against his chest. The hungry dominance of his kiss whetted her own appetite, and her arms curved around his broad shoulders to the hard muscles of his back.

Sin tasted the completeness of her response and demanded more, stimulating her to a passion that left her weak at the knees. When she was utterly his to

command, Sin untangled his mouth from her clinging, eager lips. Bewildered by his withdrawal, she
looked up at him in confusion. Her silent appeal
drew a light, totally unsatisfying kiss.

"Adam will be wondering what's happened to the
dessert," Sin offered in explanation. "We'd better
take it in to him."

Dessert? Adam? Could he possibly care about
either of them? They were the farthest things from
her mind at the moment. Only the realization of how
openly she had revealed her emotions to Sinclair
Buchanan made her withdraw from his arms.

Her hands trembled as she tried to spoon the
whipped cream onto the pumpkin pie. She felt slightly intoxicated, a warm heady glow that temporarily
cushioned her against the repercussions of her
response.

When all three slices of pie had their allotted dabs
of whipped cream, Sin picked up two of them, leaving Mara to carry her own into the dining room. She
accompanied him into the adjoining room as if in a
trance, not caring about the dessert in her hand nor
wanting to eat it. It was what he expected her to do
and she did it.

"I was beginning to wonder where you were,"
Adam commented when they appeared. "What took
so long?"

"It was my fault." It was Sin who answered,
negating the need for Mara to think of an answer. He
set one of the dessert plates in front of Adam, then
politely held out Mara's chair for her. His gaze briefly met hers, suggestively and intimately. "I was

sampling some of the cook's wares." He glanced briefly at her mouth before he turned to smile smoothly at her father.

Mara kept her eyes downcast to avoid the curious look Adam directed her way. She knew what "wares" Sin had sampled, and she hadn't yet recovered from the "sampling." It was a relief that the pie didn't require much effort to eat, because she was capable of expending little.

With the dessert finished, her father leaned back in his wheelchair. His hand patted his stomach in appreciative fullness.

"Ah, that was a delicious meal, Mara," he declared.

"There's more pie," she offered.

"I can't eat another bite. What about you, Sin?" Adam asked.

"I've had enough. And it was very good, Mara, all of it." Sin, too, extended his compliments, but in her sensitive state Mara wondered if his remark held a double meaning. It was difficult to tell. Trite phrases escaped her, so she simply nodded an acceptance.

"There is one thing I'd like," her father stated. "Coffee."

"I've made a fresh pot. Why don't the two of you have your coffee in the living room?" Mara suggested, adding hurriedly, "That way I can clear the table without stumbling over you."

"Have coffee with us first," Sin invited. "The dishes will wait. I'll help you with them later."

"No." She refused his assistance in a rush, but her hasty rejection bordered on rudeness and she tried to lessen her bluntness. "Thank you, but I don't care for any coffee right now." Rising from her chair to eliminate any discussion of her decision, she began stacking the dessert plates. "Go ahead into the living room. I'll bring your coffee directly."

As Adam rolled his chair away from the table, Mara carried the dishes into the kitchen. The kitchen door was making its pendulum swing behind her when it was pushed open. Mara glanced over he shoulder to see Sin following her with the glasses and silverware she hadn't been able to carry.

"Thanks for bringing that in." Her words were lies. The last thing she wanted was to be alone with him again.

"I told you I would help," Sin reminded her.

Hurriedly Mara arranged china cups and saucers on a tray. "Good. You can carry the coffee into the living room and save me a trip." She began filling the coffee server with the freshly brewed liquid.

"You don't need the second cup on the tray. I'm not having my coffee now," he said. "I'll have mine with you after we've cleaned everything up. Would you like me to wash or dry the dishes?"

"Neither." Her reply was abrupt. "I'd rather do it by myself. I know where everything is and where it belongs."

"You cooked the meal. It isn't fair that you have to clean up the mess afterward by yourself," he argued smoothly.

"I'm used to it. Believe me, it doesn't bother me." *Not a tenth as much as you do,* Mara thought.

"It bothers me," Sin reasoned.

"Adam would like you to have coffee with him. You're his guest," she pointed out tightly. "Please, join him in the living room. He'll enjoy your company."

"Meaning you won't?" he questioned with faint challenge.

"No." Mara added the sugar bowl and a spoon to the tray. Picking it up, she turned to face him, her gaze faltering under his disbelieving look. "Will you take this in or shall I?"

"I'll take it in." Before he did, Sin removed the second cup and set it on the counter. "But I'll be back to help."

"No." But Sin had already disappeared through the swinging door. Mara turned toward the sink with a feeling of helplessness, her teeth clenched in exasperation.

Where was her armor? What had happened to the invisible walls that usually protected her from outside forces? They seemed to have crumbled under his onslaught. Her hands gripped the edge of the kitchen counter as she sought wildly for something that would shield her from his powerful magnetism.

At the sound of footsteps approaching the door, Mara grabbed for the apron on a rack and tied it around her waist. She was at the sink filling it with water when Sin walked in.

"If you're going to do the washing, that leaves me to dry," he observed. "Where are the dish towels?"

"It's thoughtful of you to help, but I can't let you." She spoke slowly and concisely to keep her fragile control from snapping. "You're liable to get something on your suit and ruin it.'' She grasped at a straw of an excuse.

''I'll wear an apron, as you're doing.'' His calm voice sounded determined to counter her every argument.

''Don't be ridiculous!'' she flashed.

''I'm not. You are,'' he stated.

''Why don't you get it through your head that I don't want you to help me?'' she demanded, feeling the frayed edges of her nerves give way.

''Why don't you stop being so damned obstinate?'' He crooked a finger under her chin to turn her face to his.

The touch was her undoing. She jerked free of it. ''Don't you understand that I don't want to feel the way you're making me feel?'' she stormed.

''Why?'' He studied the lights blazing in her eyes with an air of curiosity. ''Because you suddenly realized you're vulnerable?''

''I don't know. And I don't care.'' Mara dismissed his suggestion as unimportant. ''I just want you to leave me alone.''

He released a breath of amusement. ''But will you promise to leave me alone?'' he challenged. ''Sexual attraction is something of a common denominator. No one is completely immune to it.''

''Sex has nothing to do with it,'' she lied.

''Not yet,'' Sin agreed.

And Mara felt herself being drawn into the force field of a powerful magnet. ''I'll buy back your lease on the cottage,'' she rushed. ''Whatever amount you say. I don't care. I want you out of it. I want you out of my life!''

Her voice had been rising in volume, in direct proportion to the panic racing through her veins. She had been so intent on the danger before her she didn't hear the whirring of the wheelchair.

Adam pushed the door to the kitchen open, frowning at the pair of them as he entered. "What's going on? You sounded as if you were shouting in here? What's the problem?"

Mara pivoted to her father her body quaking without its usual cold control. "Get him out of here!" she ordered, pointing at Sin. "Get him out of this kitchen! Out of this house!"

Shooting a questioning look at Sin, Adam's expression was both puzzled and concerned. "Sin, I think you'd better—"

"I think your daughter and I ought to thrash this out in private," Sin interrupted.

"No!" The denial exploded from Mara. "We have nothing to discuss! I don't want you here! I don't need you here!"

"That's where you're wrong." He was an immovable object, as solid as granite.

She glared at her father, daring him to take sides against her again as he had done in the past. His measured look took in her expression and the implacable features of Sin. He seemed distantly pleased by some secret thought.

"Sin, it would be best if you come with me. From past experience, I can tell you that Mara's not in a mood to listen to reason." Adam turned his chair and pointed it at the door, confident that Sin would follow him.

Sin hesitated, his flinty gaze seeming to warn Mara

that she hadn't seen or heard the last of him. Half turning, he picked up the cup and saucer sitting on the counter, the one that had been on the coffee tray.

"Adam is right." His gaze leveled on her once more before he followed her father. "Sometimes it's wiser to lose one battle in order to win the war."

As he walked out of the room, victory tasted bitter in her mouth. She turned her back on the door and closed her eyes tightly to shut out the tears. Silent, heaving sobs racked her shoulders. Her teeth bit into her lower lip to hold back any sound. Inside, everything was in a turmoil of pain, anguish and confusion.

All these turbulent emotions had become foreign to her. She had never indulged in such displays before, not even in the privacy of her room. She had kept these feelings locked away. Somehow Sin had acquired the combination. She felt as if he had just opened Pandora's box. Now that everything was being released, she wasn't sure she would be able to bring them under her control again.

The feelings Sin aroused whenever he was near her or touched her were new to her. Sexual attraction, he had called it. Mara wanted no part of it under any label. She couldn't handle the havoc it created within.

When the tempest finally subsided, Mara was weak and shaky from the storm. It took longer than usual to wash the dishes and put the kitchen back in order. Once this was accomplished, a blessed numbness enveloped her.

With its questionable protection, she abandoned

the sanctuary of the kitchen to join her father in the living room. She felt capable of confronting Sin again, unaware of the unusual pallor of her complexion or the vulnerable roundness of her eyes.

Their conversation ended the minute she entered the room, and Sin's gaze swung leisurely to encompass her. His whole bearing was one of total relaxation, leaning back in his chair, his long legs crossed. Behind his unreadable expression, Mara had the impression of alertness.

"Are you still here?" The numbness kept her voice flat and indifferent despite her challenging words. "I would have thought you'd have left by now."

"If you want some coffee, Mara," her father interceded, "I'm afraid you'll have to freshen the pot. Sin and I have pretty well emptied it."

"You should have said something about it. I would have brought you some more," she returned smoothly.

"Adam and I became engrossed in our conversation." There was a suggestion of a lazy drawl to Sin's voice as he watched her arrange their cups on the coffee tray with an air of detachment. "We were discussing a very interesting topic."

"Were you?" Her reply carried no interest in their subject matter.

"Yes, Adam and I have been talking about you and your. . .background."

His statement seemed to hover in the air before its implication began to sting. "It's bad manners to talk about people when they aren't around to defend themselves," Mara reacted in bristling defense.

"My apologies." The indolent quirk of his mouth made a mockery of his alleged sincerity. "The next time we'll make it a group therapy discussion."

"I'm not interested in your brand of therapy," she retorted, all too conscious of the forms it might take.

"Adam and I have come to the conclusion that you're something of a coward." Sin didn't even glance at her when he passed on the information. His attention was concentrated on the flame of his lighter licking the end of the cigarette between his lips.

"What?" Mara's astonishment was exceeded by her anger. She stared at her father in wordless accusation.

"It's presently only a theory," Adam offered in consolation.

"Yes," Sin agreed. "It hasn't been put to a hard test yet."

A crazy hurt was beginning to spread through her, though she tried to deny that either of the two men in the room had anything to do with it.

"I'm not interested in your theories or tests," she insisted. "Would you like some more coffee?"

"None for me, thank you," her father refused.

"I don't care for any, either." Sin exhaled a trail of smoke that drifted upward to obscure his features. "I know I'm repeating what I've said before, but the meal was delicious, Mara."

"Thank you." She tried to conceal her surprise that he had allowed her to change the subject.

"You're most welcome." There was a hint of arrogant amusement in the slight nod of his head. As Mara picked up the coffee tray to carry it to the kitchen, Sin continued, "As a matter of fact, I'd like to return your hospitality and invite you to have dinner with me on Saturday night."

She darted him a wary look, unconsciously stiffening. "Thank you, but Adam has difficulty negotiating some obstacles. We won't be able to accept your invitation."

"I wasn't inviting your father, only you," he corrected. Before she could voice the vigorous refusal forming on her tongue, Sin went on, "Adam has already given his permission for you to come. I talked to him about it first and convinced him that I could be trusted not to seduce his daughter."

A heat flamed through her that wasn't sparked by anger. "I don't care whether Adam has given his permission or not. I am not having dinner with you. There would be absolutely no point to it."

As Mara started toward the kitchen with the tray, Sin rose to his feet with a lithe swiftness and blocked her path. He seemed to tower impregnably before her, too broad to sidestep.

"You're forgetting one point. There was something you wanted to discuss with me," he reminded her.

"Oh?" Her knees threatened to buckle. "I don't recall wanting to talk to you about anything." Her air of bravado was quickly deserting her.

"Don't you?" His eyes were half-closed against the smoke from his cigarette, but it didn't lessen their sharpness. "It was something to do with the cottage and when I would be leaving it."

Her gaze fell under the dominance of his. "Yes,

well, it's a discussion that doesn't have to take place over dinner. In fact it should take place here, not at the cottage.''

Sin appeared to loom closer. ''Saturday night at six o'clock, at the cottage, is the only time I'll discuss my terms for leaving.''

''That's blackmail!'' Mara breathed out the accusal.

''I suppose you could call it that,'' he agreed, and bent to stub out his cigarette in an ashtray near Adam's wheelchair. ''Unless you're a coward, you'll be there.'' He ignored her openmouthed look of indignation and addressed her father. ''It's time I was leaving, Adam. I enjoyed talking to you. Happy Thanksgiving.'' The last parting phrase was issued to both of them.

Mara still hadn't found her voice when the front door closed behind Sin. She turned to her father, who was looking at her with something akin to sympathy. His expression didn't endear him to her.

''I am not going to dinner with him, regardless of his attempt to blackmail me into coming.'' She said to Adam what she would have told Sin if he hadn't left.

''That's your decision.'' Her father shrugged, indicating he wasn't going to argue or try to persuade her into accepting.

''What was the idea of giving him permission to ask me to dinner?'' Mara demanded. ''I'm of legal age. I don't require your permission.''

''I didn't exactly give my permission,'' he corrected. ''Sin asked me if I had any objections to being alone for a couple of hours on Saturday night because he wanted to have dinner with you alone. I merely told him I didn't object and that you were free to go out with him if you wished.''

"Well, I don't wish," she snapped. "And what's all this nonsense about convincing you he wouldn't seduce me?''

"I think it was an attempt on his part to assure both of us that, despite first impressions, he's an honorable man," he answered, referring to Sin's female companionship the first couple of weekends in the cottage. "I'd already guessed he was a man of his word. He said he wouldn't seduce you on Saturday night and I believe him.''

"He isn't going to get the chance," she retorted, and immediately sought to clarify a point. "Not going doesn't mean I'm a coward, either.''

"If you say so." Adam's skeptical tone didn't indicate that he agreed with her.

"I'm not a coward," Mara repeated angrily.

"There's an easy way to prove it." Using one wheel as a pivot point, Adam turned his chair around. "I think I'll watch the football game in my room.''

After he had pushed himself out of the room, there was no one left for Mara to argue with except herself. But there was little desire left to argue.

CHAPTER EIGHT

PULLING THE COLLAR of her parka tighter around her neck, Mara paused to stare at the lighted windows of the cottage. It was cold with the threat of snow in the air. She had never admitted to being nervous about anything, but she was now.

Half a dozen times during her walk to the cottage she had been on the verge of fleeing back to the house. But Sin's taunt that she would be a coward if she didn't come to dinner kept driving her on. Mara realized that he had known it would. She was playing into his hands, trapped by circumstances that would permit her to do nothing else.

Shivering from the cold and nerves, she walked the last few feet to the door and knocked twice. A mass of butterflies fluttered in her stomach. She took a deep, calming breath in the hope of quieting them. The door opened and immediately swung wide to admit her. Shakily expelling the breath she had taken in, Mara walked in.

Sin's bulk intimidated her more than it ever had before. Her gaze glanced over him. A white roll-neck sweater of heavy ribbed weave covered the width and breadth of his torso. Black slacks gave added length to his legs.

A fire cracked in the fireplace. Except for one dim lamp, it provided the only light in the living room. The mantle clock chimed the hour.

"Right on time," Sin observed. "You're punctual."

"Yes." Mara couldn't shake of the feeling that she was a lamb being led into the den of a silver-tipped wolf.

His hand reached toward her and she backed away from it instinctively, her gaze flying to his face in alarm. His mouth slanted in amusement.

"May I take your coat?" he offered.

And Mara realized he had only intended to help her out of it. Fighting the self-conscious waves of foolishness, she fumbled with the buttons. Her chilled fingers weren't very cooperative. When at last they had completed the task, she started to shrug out of the coat. Sin's hands were there to help her, brushing her shoulders and sending tingles of awareness down her spine.

"Thank you," she murmured so he wouldn't guess his assistance had caused any disturbance.

A strong sense of self-preservation made her notice where Sin had put her coat. It was draped over a hook on the hall tree near the door, a new addition of furniture to the cottage.

"How do you like your steak cooked?" Sin inquired.

"Well done," Mara responded automatically.

Again a smile teased the corners of his strong mouth. "Somehow I guessed that."

He surveyed her coatless frame. The frankly sensual look prompted Mara to hug her arms across her stomach. She wasn't dressed in any way suggestively, but Sin made her feel she was.

Her slacks and loose top were peacock blue, tailored and not at all clinging. Her fingers made an unconscious inspection of the buttons of her cream silk blouse to be sure they were all fastened. They were. Ill at ease, she lifted her chin and tried to shake away the uncomfortable sensation.

"May I fix you a drink?" It was the polite inquiry of a host, but it didn't mask the light dancing in his eyes.

"Nothing, thank you," Mara refused, steadfast in her determination to have her wits about her this evening.

"Would you excuse me, then?" Sin asked, "I put the steaks in the broiler a few minutes ago and I'd better check them. You can have a seat in the living room, if you like, or come along with me to the kitchen."

One glance at the dimly lit living room and the intimate feeling it evoked decided Mara's mind. The kitchen was infinitely better lighted than the living room. She opted for it.

"I'll come with you if you don't mind," she said.

"Skeptical that I can really cook a meal?" he jested, but didn't exact a reply.

Sin entered the kitchen, aware that Mara followed, but he paid no attention to her as he checked the steaks in the broiler. The small table held two place settings. Wooden bowls of tossed salad sat at each place, along with cut-glass wine goblets.

"Unless you would prefer to wait, we can have our salad now." He straightened from the broiler and noticed her preoccupation with the wineglasses. "I hope you like wine with your meal."

"Champagne?" Mara heard herself question dryly, her thoughts turning to the day he had first arrived when Celene had brought in a bottle of champagne.

His gaze slid over her, remembering, too. "No, you don't strike me as the champagne type," he answered in a voice dry with silent humor. "Something staid and prosaic like hearty burgundy seems more your line."

He produced a decanter of wine and filled the two glasses with the deep red liquid. After setting them on the table, he held out a chair for her.

"About the cottage," Mara began, wanting to get to the objective of her visit.

"I never discuss business before or during a meal," he stated.

Impatience surged through her, but she was determined not to give rise to it. She sat down in the chair Sin offered and tried to ignore the brief contact with his hand as he pushed the chair to the table. While he was sitting down at the opposite end of the narrow table, she shook out her linen napkin and spread it across her lap.

"I hope you like the dressing on the salad. It's a special concoction of mine," Sin informed her. "Italian with variations."

She sampled the lettuce salad. "It's very good," she admitted, trying to be the courteous guest.

"The secret is the dill flakes," he confided. "They give the dressing that touch of piquancy."

"Oh." Mara was having difficulty adjusting to this kind of conversation. She was accustomed to battling his taunting remarks or personal comments. This casual small talk was putting her off stride. She sensed he knew it, too.

After a couple of minutes Sin rose from his chair to check the steak. The succulent aroma coming from the broiler was decidedly appetizing. Mara, who had thought she wouldn't be able to eat a bit, felt the first pangs of hunger.

"You're an excellent cook," Sin observed when he was reseated at the table. "Do you like to cook?"

"I've never thought of it in terms of liking it or disliking it." The prongs of her fork rested in the salad bowl as she considered his question, surprised to find she didn't have a ready answer. "It's always been something that had to be done. But yes, I think I enjoy it. Do you?"

"I wouldn't if I had to do it every day, but it's a form of relaxation for me."

"What do you do when you're in Baltimore? Do you mostly eat at restaurants or—" She glanced at his left hand. Just because he hadn't been married to Celene as she had first supposed, it didn't mean he wasn't married, or hadn't been married. Mara realized there was a great deal she didn't know about him—his background, his work, his interests, anything.

He saw the direction of her glance and guessed the reason her question wasn't finished. The grooves

carved on either side of his mouth became more in-
grained as he tried to conceal a knowing smile.

"I'm not married. Did you think I had an understanding wife waiting patiently in Baltimore for me
to return from the Thanksgiving holidays?" Sin
arched her a taunting look. "I can't imagine any
woman being that understanding."

Mara admitted to herself that he was right. "You
could be divorced or separated...." She pointed out
the possibilities.

"Neither, I'm a widower. My wife was a dystroph-
ic. She died seven years ago." His voice remained
completely conversational, registering no sorrow.

"I'm sorry." She felt obliged to voice some sympathy. But she looked at him anew, trying to
visualize the circumstances of his marriage and his
attitude toward a wife with rapidly deteriorating
health. How had he reacted, she wondered.

"I was aware of Ann's condition when I married
her," Sin answered her unspoken question.

Startled, Mara blurted, "Then why did you marry
her?"

"Because I cared for her," he answered simply. "I
wanted to look after her and see that she had the best
help possible."

His response was discomfiting. She didn't want to
believe his motives. Her fork attacked the last bit of
salad in the bowl.

"You could have done that without the noble gesture of marriage." Her reply was stiff, tinged with
sarcasm.

"It wouldn't have fulfilled my sense of obligation

and duty. Ann didn't have anyone else. You should know about that, Mara. You could have paid for Adam's care, rather than take him into your home." Deftly Sin deflected her comment, the calm pitch of his voice unchanging.

"The situations don't compare," she retorted.

"Don't they?" His gaze skimmed her face as he murmured a thought aloud: "I seem to continually collect lost souls." Then his gaze flicked to her empty salad bowl. "Are you finished?"

"Yes, thank you." Mara sat rigidly in her chair as Sin rose to clear the dishes.

The steaks were done. He set a plate before Mara containing a generous cut of browned beef and a baked potato, butter melting in its split jacket. A bright garnish of sliced apple rings rested in a corner.

"To answer your previous question, I eat out occasionally when I'm in Baltimore." Sin resumed their conversation as he sat down. "I have a housekeeper and cook on staff, so I generally have my meals at home. Part of the appeal of coming here to the cottage each weekend is the fact that there's no one around to wait on me. That and privacy as well as the freedom to work without interruption."

"What kind of work do you do? I know you're the head of some company." Mara remembered that from Harve Bennett's investigations before she leased Sin the cottage.

"It's a minor conglomerate with a variety of enterprises under its wing. My work is mainly in administration and organization, a desk job with challenges."

Mara sensed that his reply was an understatement.

There was no reference to the tremendous power he commanded or the pressure of high finance. She had no doubt that he handled both with ease. His personality was too marked with self-assurance.

"My father started the company," Sin continued, pausing to sip his wine. "I inherited it from him when he passed away a few years ago."

The information didn't surprise her. Mara had suspected his wealth wasn't newly acquired. His indifference to the cost of things, this cottage for instance, indicated that he was accustomed to having what he wanted, regardless of the price.

She also guessed, "You took over the company and enlarged it?" He had too much drive to be content with the status quo of things.

Over the rim of his wineglass his blue eyes briefly met hers. "I have expanded it, yes," Sin admitted, but with the attitude that this was an unimportant fact.

The information she was receiving about him was being filed in a haphazard order and merely whetted her curiosity to know more. The food on her plate was being consumed without her being conscious of its delicious taste or quantity.

"Why did you spend Thanksgiving here? With your father gone, don't you have any other family?" Mara questioned.

"I have some cousins on the West Coast and an aunt and uncle, but no brothers or sisters. My mother died suddenly of a heart attack when I was in college." He seemed not to mind her personal questions. "If I'd stayed in Baltimore, Ginger, my cook, would have insisted on fixing a big dinner with all the trimmings. It would have been a total waste for one person. So instead I gave my staff the week off to spend the holidays with their own families, and came here." He glanced at her across the table, an attractive smile curving his well-defined mouth. "As it turned out, I had an excellently prepared Thanksgiving dinner anyway and the pleasure of Adam's company and yours."

Her pulse hammered slightly—whether from his smile or his reference to the pleasure he found in her company, she wasn't sure.

"What do you find to do here, besides jogging, I mean? Aren't you bored?" Mara took a sip of her wine, surprised to find more than half of it gone.

"I do a lot of thinking and planning, dictate correspondence and memos, and go over reports and balance sheets. Mostly I relax." Sin refilled her glass and his own. "Tonight, with you, will probably turn out to be one of the livelier evenings I've spent here."

The others must have been spent with Celene, Mara concluded. "Why don't you bring Miss Taylor here anymore?" she wondered aloud.

"Taken in small doses, Celene's company can be stimulating," he explained dryly. "But over a long period, her attractions begin to pall."

"Too many 'Sin, darlings'?" Mara intended it as a taunt, but it sounded more like a teasing exchange between friends.

"Something like that," Sin agreed, his lazy glance not revealing that he found anything unusual in her new tone. "How was your steak?"

"It was very good." She had eaten it all, not toying with it once from nervousness. "Where did you learn to cook?"

"I picked it up here and there, mostly by trial and error during college. It's a skill that comes in handy when a business meeting stretches until midnight. I don't have to wake anyone up to fix me a meal."

"Does that happen often?" Mara asked.

"Often enough." Sin finished his dinner and straightened from his chair. He took her plate, stacked it on top of his and set it on the sink counter. "Dessert is a plate of assorted fruits and cheeses. I thought we'd have it with the rest of the wine in the living room. I'll clear the table first."

"I'll help you," she volunteered.

"No." He refused her assistance flatly. "You wouldn't let me help you Thanksgiving, so you can't help me tonight. I'll just put them in the sink and wash them later."

His reminder had the desired effect of keeping Mara in her seat while he smoothly and efficiently cleared the table. In the interim, her self-consciousness returned and she felt stiff and ill at ease again. There was a rigidity to her carriage when she rose and carried her wineglass into the living room. Sin followed with the dessert plate and his own wineglass.

The dimness of the living room immediately enveloped Mara in a feeling of intimacy. The fire had died to red embers amid a bed of charcoal-gray ashes, almost the same color as Sin's hair. He set the dessert plate on the wood-inlaid surface of a small serving table in front of the davenport. Mara stood nervously to one side, the cozy atmosphere too much for her.

"Help yourself." Sin gestured toward the fruit and cheese and walked over to add wood to the fire.

Hesitantly Mara took a cube of cheese and nibbled at it. The empty cusions of the davenport were too inviting and the chairs seemed too pointedly isolated. So she remained standing, her shoes sinking into the lush pile of the alpaca rug, while Sin knelt in front of the hearth, poking the embers into flames around the new fuel. Amid all the questions she'd asked him, one came back to her now—the one he hadn't answered.

"About the cottage..." she began as she had before. "When will you be leaving?"

Sin didn't turn around. "When my lease expires next fall."

"But—"

"You signed the contract." He straightened as the fire flickered and blazed. "I expect you to honor the conditions it contains. You were the one who insisted on a year's lease," he reminded her.

"But I thought I was here to discuss when you would vacate." Mara completed the sentence she had begun earlier.

"We've discussed it and I've told you under what conditions I will be vacating the cottage," he replied calmly.

"You had no intention ever, of terminating the lease early, did you?" she accused in a chilling voice. "You only let me think you would."

"No, there was nothing to discuss as far as I was

concerned, but you didn't come here about the cottage. You came because you didn't want to be considered a coward,'' Sin concluded without a trace of doubt.

"I'm not a coward!" Her fingers gripped the stem of her wineglass so tightly that it was in danger of snapping.

He turned his back to the fireplace, the flames crackling and popping over the bark of the new logs. He made no move toward her, although his gaze was on her.

"Adam and I talked a lot about that while you were washing dishes the other day. We talked about many things," he added.

"I can imagine the biased stories he told you," Mara returned bitterly.

"He explained to me how much his divorce from your mother had hurt you." His features were shadowed by the back light of the fire, but she felt the intensity of his gaze.

"Hurt me?" She was incredulous at the statement. "It crippled my mother. Did he neglect to mention that?"

"Don't you believe he cared?" Sin questioned.

"I believe in the fickleness of men," she retorted, and walked to the fireplace to stare into the fire's yellow flames licking hungrily over its wooden food.

"I first thought you'd built those invisible walls around you so people couldn't get close to you. I was half right," he observed. "You want to keep everybody away so they'll never be able to hurt you.

You're determined not to care about people because they might leave you the way your father did."

"Don't you think that's wise?" Mara challenged, and took a sip of wine to show her indifference to his remarks.

"It may be wise, but it's hopelessly impossible." After sending her a sideways glance, Sin moved to stand behind her. "You can't roll all your emotions and feelings, passions and desires into a neat little bundle and stuff them in your hind pocket."

Mara hugged and arm across her stomach, trying to ward off her awareness of how close he was to her. She was conscious of the height and breadth of him and felt the warmth of his body, although no part of him was touching her.

"Even if you could," he continued, "your body is designed to perform certain biological functions that respond to outside stimuli." His hands curved onto her slender waist. When Mara tried to step away, their hold tightened. "It doesn't matter whether you want to feel the way I make you. It's a reaction of our two chemistries."

"Sexual attraction." She referred to the term he had used before, a breathlessness to her words.

"Yes. It doesn't do any good to fight it." He reached around her to take the wineglass from her unresisting fingers and set it on the mantelpiece.

She was drawn backward until her shoulders were against his chest and her hips felt his solidly muscled thighs. The outline of his hard male frame seemed to burn its impression into her. It started quicksilver fires that flamed through her limbs. His arms overlapped across the front of her stomach, his fingers spreading across her rib cage below her breasts. An aching tension twisted her stomach in knots.

Her hands crossed each other to seek his wrists. When they found them, she could only hold them in the same position. The thought of removing them had fled the minute her fingers felt the wisps of masculine hair growing on his arm. Her sensitive nerve ends vibrated with the sensual contact.

His head was bent toward hers, his jaw and chin brushing near her ear, his warm breath stirring the silken shortness of her dark hair. The scent of him was a mixture of wine and smoke and the heady fragrance of an elusive cologne. Her heart tripped wildly against her ribs. She closed her eyes against the quaking reaction of her senses to Sin, but the darkness only increased his potency.

"It's natural for my touch to excite you." His voice was pitched low, soothing in its warmth and disturbing in its huskiness. "It's a physical response that has nothing to do with what your mind wants. You have to learn to separate the two."

But the thought of him was dominating her mind, too. There wasn't room for anything else. He crowded into every nook of her being, dominating it until she could only shake her head in dazed protest.

"When will it stop?" she wanted to know.

"The only cure I know for sexual attraction is prolonged exposure." His mouth explored the side of her neck, sending delicious shivers over her sensitive skin. "Tonight can be the beginning of a series of experiments."

"Yes," Mara agreed, her voice hardly above a whisper.

Sin nuzzled her ear, his strong teeth gently nipping at the lobe. The caress unleashed a torrent of reactions. She melted against him, his outline more sharply defined against her curves. An arm was removed from around her as his mouth lingered near her ear, then moved away.

"Here's your wine," he said in a prompting voice.

In confusion, Mara blinked at the glass he held. She had no desire for wine, but he seemed to want her to take it. She took it from his hand to hold it unsteadily in her own. A second later Sin was bending and lifting her off her feet. Her arm automatically curved around his neck as he carried her effortlessly to the couch. There he sat down, cradling her on his lap.

"Drink up." His hand closed around her fingers holding the glass and moved it toward her lips. At her apprehensive look, a faint smile alleviated the firmness of his mouth. "Don't worry, I'm not trying to get you drunk. But the wine will help you relax."

His reasoning made sense. Mara knew a fine-boned tension was making her hold herself stiffly in his lap. She kept wondering if she was too heavy or if he was comfortable in this position.

With dark smoky blue eyes he watched her sip the wine. His fingers slid partially down her hand, his thumb rubbing the inside of her wrist and making exciting forays to her sensitive palm. When she lowered the glass from her mouth, his gaze studied her lips, faintly moist from the wine.

"We need to get you used to being touched and held first before we can graduate to other things," Sin told her huskily. The mantel clock chimed the quarter hour and Mara started guiltily, only to be restrained by his arm. "Do you see what I mean?" He gave her a lazy look filled with knowledge.

Leaning slightly forward, he reached for the dessert plate on the serving table and set it on the seat cushion beside them. Mara watched him separate a pale green grape from its cluster and offer it to her.

"Have a grape," he suggested. "It's the seedless variety, so you don't have to be concerned about how you're going to dispose of the seeds." He carried it to her lips and hesitantly she let him slide it into her mouth. The brush of his fingers evoked provocative thoughts. "Good?"

"Yes." But Mara was struggling with a whole new set of erotic sensations.

"Have another." This time Sin offered her the cluster so she could pluck her own grape.

At his insistence, Mara ate two more. When she took the fourth he set the cluster on the plate and captured her hand before she placed the grape in her mouth. Instead, he carried it to his own. Her fingers trembled as they touched his mouth to slide the grape inside. Her pulse raced madly through her veins from the sensuous implication of her actions.

After that the grapes were divided between them and Sin took sips from her wine. Once he kissed her, the taste of grapes and wine mingling together with their lips. Her position on his lap became more natural; in spite of its intimacy, she became more relaxed.

When the wine was gone, Sin put the glass and the dessert plate on the table. The emptiness of her hands made them feel useless until Sin found a purpose for them. He cupped one to his face, kissing the palm, then letting it slide along his jaw.

Her breath became choked off by the sudden tightening of her throat as his head slowly bent to hers. The kiss that followed was a leisurely exercise. Instead of Mara having to feel her way through her relative lack of experience, Sin was showing her the way.

It was a long, slow process and Sin was teaching her to enjoy every minute of it. Meanwhile his hands were caressing her, wandering over her hips and thighs and gliding over her spine. Their touch aroused her at an unhurried tempo.

The intoxicating pleasure of his possessing kisses was a heady thing. Gradually they sent raw desire spreading through her veins, heating her flesh to a fever warmth. Sin molded her according to his will. Nothing registered in her mind but the aching needs and wants he was instilling in her.

Unerring fingers found the buttons of her blouse, and she shifted on his lap in faint protest. Not forcing the issue, Sin bent his head to kiss her throat. His hand covered a breast, the rounded flesh swelling firm under his touch. The silk of her blouse was no barrier, she realized.

Sensing her acquiescence, Sin efficiently but unhurriedly unfastened the buttons. Seconds later, the lacy engineering of her bra was disposed of and her soft flesh was spilling into his hand. His lips made a breathtaking investigation of the new territory. Dizzying excitement thundered through her veins as she shuddered from sheer rapture.

It was a new world for her, with fresh discoveries to be made at every turn. His power over her grew stronger instead of weaker during the prolonged exposure. When his mouth returned to take passionate command of her lips, she submitted, surrendered and returned his fire.

The innocent lovemaking showed her the glorious promise of the real thing, made her eager to know the wonder of it, but her teacher was repeating the same lessons, wisely not rushing her. And Mara didn't object.

The chimes from the clock sounded again. She had grown used to their softly ringing tones, having mixed them up several times with the sound of bells ringing in her head. But they distracted Sin's attention.

His mouth lingered on her lips an instant longer. Then his hand was stroking her cheek as he drew away. His eyes were darkly blue as they met the passionately disturbed light in hers. He took a deep breath, seemingly in an attempt to control his own inclinations.

"I promised Adam I'd have you home by ten," he told her, and glanced briefly at his watch. "That gives us only half an hour."

Ten o'clock. Adam. Promise. The words echoed through her mind, its thought processes slowed.

While Mara tried to surface from the irresistible tide of desire, Sin began fixing her clothes, fastening clasps and buttons. Irritation born of her unsatisfied condition made her move shakily off his lap.

"Next I suppose that you'll tell me you aren't going to complete your seduction of me because of the other promise you gave Adam." Her voice was remarkably steady as she released her frustration in a taunting accusal.

Sin was on his feet, taking her by the shoulders and turning her to face him. He caught her downcast chin between his fingers and tilted it back to examine her face. Her eyes glimmered with mingled mutiny and regret.

"I have no intention of ever seducing you, Mara," he told her, and pain stabbed through her with the sharp breath she took. The firm line of his sensual mouth softened. "I will never persuade you to let me make love to you against your will."

Realizing how much of her innermost feelings she had betrayed, Mara turned away from him, mumbling, "I'll get my coat." She walked swiftly to the hall tree on which Sin had hung her coat.

He followed but made no attempt to help her on with her coat as he took his own from a hook. "Instead of taking the car, I'll walk you home," he said. "I think we can both benefit from the cold air."

Mara didn't argue. She readily admitted to herself that she needed something to cool her flesh and her senses. She couldn't find any consolation in the fact that Sin apparently felt the same way.

Once they were both outside the cottage, Sin produced a flashlight from his pocket. The brilliant beam picked out the track through the woods and led the way. They followed it in silence, the frosty air nipping at their faces and turning their breath into vaporous clouds.

When the lights of the house came in sight, Sin spoke. "I'll be leaving for Baltimore tomorrow. I won't be back until next weekend, probably very late Friday night."

Mara continued walking toward the back door, staring straight ahead. "Don't forget to leave a list of what you'll be needing."

The flashlight went off as his hand stopped her and turned her to face him. "Don't forget what you've learned."

His mouth crushed down on hers, hard and punishing. Its fierceness stole her breath and inflamed her senses. The walk had chilled none of her desire. Just as quickly as it had begun, the kiss was ended and Sin was striding into the night.

CHAPTER NINE

THE FOLLOWING SATURDAY Mara had finished washing the breakfast dishes and was pottering around the kitchen. She didn't stray far from the window above the sink. Sin would have arrived at the cottage sometime last night, she knew. Her anticipation at seeing him again was running high, partly with eagerness and partly with apprehension.

As she went past the window, her gaze was drawn beyond its panes. A familiar silver-gray car was stopping in the driveway to park beside the house. Her heart gave a little leap and she turned guiltily away from the window. She didn't want to admit that she had been watching for him.

Quickly she sought an excuse for being in the kitchen. Taking a mug from the cupboard, she walked to the coffeepot. As the car door slammed, Mara kept her back to the door so she could pretend she didn't know he was coming. The thick walls of the house prevented her from hearing his footsteps. She could only wait for the knock on the door.

Sin entered without knocking. The only advance warning Mara had was the sound of the doorknob turning, and in the next second he was in the kitchen.

She turned with a start to be regarded lazily by the cloudy darkness of his blue eyes.

"Hello, Mara." The warmth of his low greeting was disturbing.

Unable to respond naturally, she turned back to the coffeepot. "I was just going to pour a cup of coffee. Would you like some?" Her polite inquiry was stilted, almost as betraying as the knocking of her knees.

"No, I don't want any coffee." The sound of his voice came closer and Mara knew he was walking toward her. Her silly heart skipped a beat, then rocketed when his hands slid around her waist. "And neither do you."

The breath she took became more of a gasp as Sin nuzzled the side of her neck. "Where's Adam?" He spoke against her skin.

"In the other room." Her voice wavered under the spell of his caress.

Sin turned her sideways in his arms, her shoulder against his chest and her hip pressed against the strong column of his thighs. Curving a hand along the side of her neck, he tilted her chin with his thumb. His mouth closed over hers, parting her lips with sweet intensity. When the coolness of uncertainty ended and Mara responded, the kiss lingered for an instant before Sin raised his head. His thumb made a feather tracing of her warm, trembling lips.

"I told you not to forget," he murmured. He released her from the intoxicating circle of his arms to take hold of her hand. "Let's find Adam."

"Why?" Mara asked in confusion.

But Sin didn't bother to answer as he led her from the kitchen. Adam was in his study, taking notes from the diary of a rebel soldier. He glanced up when they entered, his gaze dancing to Mara's hand held firmly in Sin's.

"Hello, Sin." He seemed not at all surprised by the scene he was viewing.

"Have you made any plans for today, Adam?" Sin asked, ignoring Mara's attempt to wiggle her hand free.

"No. Should I?" Her father was trying hard not to smile.

"I'm taking Mara away for the day," Sin explained further. "I've never been to the Amish country around Lancaster, so I'm going to make use of her services as a guide. We'll be gone for the better part of the day and I know she won't want to leave you alone that long."

Mara stared openmouthed at the announcement. She couldn't think of even a halfhearted protest. She was being swept along in the tidal force of Sin's presence and had no desire to save herself.

"No problem," Adam assured them with a shrug. "Sam Jenkins will come over. Since he's retired, he welcomes any excuse to get out of the house."

"Give him a call while Mara gets ready," Sin suggested, and glanced at her. "How long will it take you? I'll give you ten minutes and no more." Before Mara could take a breath, she was being turned toward the staircase in the foyer.

With the ten-minute time limit, she didn't have time to consider whether going with Sin was something she wanted to do. She changed out of her slacks into a wool skirt of winter white and pulled a complementing sweater of French-blue angora over her head. Pausing only to fluff her hair with her fingertips, she hurried back downstairs.

"Ready?" Sin had her coat and scarf in hand.

Mara glanced at her father, who answered the unspoken question in her dark eyes. "Sam is on his way over here. Don't worry about me, I'll be fine."

"There's vegetable stew in the refrigerator. Have Sam warm it for your lunch," she instructed as Sin helped her on with her coat. "And there's some cold cuts for sandwiches."

"We'll find plenty to eat," Adam replied. "Sam is good at raiding a refrigerator."

The arm around Mara's shoulders firmly guided her to the front door so that no more time was wasted with last-minute instructions. Outside, Sin walked her to the passenger door of his car.

"I'll drive," he explained, helping her inside. "That way I'll have something to concentrate on besides you." His look was darkly blue and meaningful, throwing her more off balance than she already was.

Trying to hide the exciting confusion she felt, Mara glanced back at the house when Sin slid behind the wheel of the car. "Do you think Adam will be all right?" she asked.

"Instead of thinking about Adam, maybe you should be wondering if you'll be all right...with me." His glance was teasing.

"Will I?" Mara was stunned by the provocative question that came from her lips.

This time when his gaze met hers, it was quietly considering, a bit probing in its attention. "It all depends on whether you're better at being a guide than a distraction." His gaze swung away from her as he turned the car onto the graveled road. "We'll soon find out if you're as knowledgeable about the Pennsylvania Dutch as you were about Gettysburg."

"I do know the term 'Pennsylvania Dutch' has nothing to do with Holland. They're descended from German immigrants. The word 'Dutch' is an American corruption of '*deutsch*', and '*Deutschland*' is the German homeland," Mara responded with an almost euphoric feeling of self-confidence that was strange under the circumstances.

"That's a good start." Sin flashed a brief smile in her direction.

Mara looked out the window at the crisp blue day. It was too perfect to be marred by anything. The feeling remained with her throughout the day.

When they arrived at the Lancaster area, she guided him onto the side roads, away from the commercialism of the main highway. The information she relayed about the area was never given as a means of defense; it flowed naturally and freely from her.

They lunched at a local restaurant specializing in Pennsylvania Dutch dishes. Even when Sin mildly flirted with her, she never felt threatened by his advances. On tours in the area, they walked hand in hand or he curved an arm around her shoulders. The action seemed part of the natural order of things.

After midafternoon Sin turned the car toward Gettysburg and home. Mara sat close to him, his arm around her shoulders, her head resting against his shoulder. Contentment warmed and relaxed her.

Sam Jenkins was just leaving when they arrived at the house. Adam insisted he hadn't been aware of Mara's absence; his day had been too full. It was Adam who invited Sin to stay for dinner, an invitation that Mara seconded. Sin didn't need any persuading to accept.

Afterward her father and Sin played chess in the living room while Mara washed the dishes. Adam had just scored a checkmate when she entered the living room. He was leaning back in his wheelchair, a knowing smile on his face.

"I don't think your mind was on the game, Sin," her father declared. "That win was almost too easy."

"You could be right," Sin acknowledged, his gaze sliding to Mara as if she was somehow the cause of his loss.

She hadn't even been in the room, so it seemed illogical that she was to blame for his lack of attentiveness to the game. Still, the implied compliment made her feel all warm and shaky inside.

"How about some hot chocolate?" she suggested.

"Sounds good," her father was the first to agree. "Only I'll have mine in my room. It's been a long day and I'm beginning to feel the effects."

He didn't look tired. In fact, Mara had the fleeting thought that she had never seen him looking more alert. But such impressions were often misleading, or at least Mara was willing to pretend they were since it meant being alone with Sin.

"I'll help you, Adam," Sin offered before Mara

had a chance to step forward, "while Mara makes the cocoa."

His logic defied protest and Mara found herself returning to the kitchen she had vacated only moments ago. It didn't take long to heat the milk, and pour it over the cocoa and sugar in the mugs. Marshmallows bobbed and melted on top of the steaming liquid as she carried the tray of mugs into the living room. She left two mugs there and carried the third on the tray to her father.

When she entered the bedroom, Sin retreated to let them say their good-nights in private. Her father was in bed. Mara set the tray on the bedside table within his reach.

"Sin mentioned that you had a good time today," Adam commented.

"Yes, it's been a while since I've been in Lancaster. It was interesting." Her response was deliberately noncommittal. Her emotional reaction toward Sin was too new to be discussed openly, and certainly not with her father. "Good night, Adam."

"Good night."

Soft music was being played on the radio in the living room. Sin turned as she entered and held out a hand to her in silent invitation. Mara hesitated, aware suddenly of the limitation of her experience.

"I don't dance very well," she told him.

"It isn't necessary for you to know," he returned.

With casual purpose, he crossed the distance necessary to reach her hand and draw her into his arms. It seemed she had waited all day to be in his embrace, so naturally did her body fit itself to his.

The hand at the back of her waist guided her to the slow tempo of the music in swaying steps that required little concentration. Mara was capable of little. An avalanche of sensations seemed to tumble on top of her. The lower half of her body was welded to his hard, muscled thighs, his heat burning her. His gaze roamed possessively over her upturned face, its look sending her senses spinning into orbit.

The smell of him, the feel of him was boldly male and rawly disturbing. Sin carried her hand to his mouth, his white teeth nibbling at her sensitive fingertips. She lost all awareness of the music playing in the background. When he opened her hand to press a kiss into its palm, her limbs quivered. The sensual probing of his tongue against its hollow released a shuddering sigh of surrender from her throat.

All pretense of dancing ended as Sin's mouth sought her ready lips, taking them with languid passion. A blind, unending yearning had her trembling in his arms. His caressing hands made a slow intimate exploration of her shape, their leisurely investigation kindling a hotter fire between them.

At some point they must have gravitated toward the nearest chair, because when Mara surfaced briefly she was on his lap. His deliberate and total mastery of her senses had turned her into modeling clay, and she could think of nothing more exquisite than to be shaped according to his will.

There was a ragged edge to his breathing as Sin ended a lingering kiss. Her hand curved along his chiseled jaw to draw him back, but he resisted her appeal, a bemused yet firm light in his charcoal-blue eyes.

"The hot chocolate is getting cold," he murmured.

"I don't care," Mara admitted with a total lack of inhibition.

He removed his hand from beneath her sweater and turned her so that her feet were on the floor. "Neither do I, but I think you'd better reheat it just the same." Ignoring her resistance, Sin stood her up and pushed her toward the kitchen as he rose from the chair.

Reluctantly Mara took their hot chocolate into the kitchen and warmed it. Sin joined her within a few minutes. They talked of trivial things and avoided any reference to the passionate embrace in the living room. Before he left, Sin kissed her good-night and said he'd see her in the morning.

THAT WEEKEND became the pattern for the weekends that followed. Almost every waking moment was spent together. Some part of the weekend included a few hours away from the farmhouse, either touring a local point of interest or having dinner. For Mara, the weekdays were spent waiting for the weekend and Sin's arrival.

The weekend before Christmas arrived on the heels of a snowstorm. On Saturday morning Mara waited anxiously for Sin to appear at the house, wondering if he had even driven up the night before on the snowy roads. She had made a dozen trips to the window above the sink for a glimpse of him.

As she started toward it again, Adam remarked, "A watched pot never boils."

Self-consciously Mara turned away before reaching her destination, and murmured a stilted, "I don't know what you're talking about."

"You don't, huh?" he teased with a half smile. "My mistake. I thought you were looking for Sin."

She glanced at the kitchen wall clock. "That's right. He usually is at the house by this time, isn't he?" she replied as if it was the first time she had realized it.

This ploy didn't fool her father. "Mara, I'm not blind." He shook his head and smiled. "For three consecutive weekends you two have been inseparable. I'm getting used to losing my daughter at the weekends. If you're worried about Sin, why don't you walk down to the cottage and see if he's there?"

She abandoned her pretense of mild interest to ask, "Do you think I should?"

"Anything is better than having you pace the floor like an expectant father," Adam replied.

Mara hesitated, torn between the aggressiveness of such an action and her anxiety. Finally she started for the coat rack where her parka was hung.

"I think I will," she decided.

"If he's there, don't hurry back on my account," her father told her, watching indulgently as she hurriedly put on her coat.

Half of the buttons were fastened when the back door opened and Sin walked in. Mara turned, her face lighting up at the sight of him. At the slightest invitation from him she would have run into his arms.

A shutter seemed to close over his gaze as he noted

her expression. Sin swung his attention to her father, a smile of greeting touching his mouth.

"Hello, Adam." He spoke to her father first, then glanced at her. "Were you going somewhere?"

His aura of aloofness kept Mara from admitting her destination. "Just for a walk." Hurt twinged through her as she began unbuttoning her coat. "The coffee is fresh. Would you like a cup?"

"Please." Sin walked to the table and sat in a chair near her father.

While she hung up her coat and poured him a cup of coffee, the two men discussed the weather and the condition of the roads. Mara took a chair opposite Sin at the table. He smiled at her once, but continued conversing with her father.

"One thing is for sure—we're going to have a white Christmas this year. This snow isn't going to melt in five days," Adam stated. "Will you be staying over until after Christmas, Sin?"

"No, I have to drive back to Baltimore tomorrow afternoon, but I'll be back on Christmas Eve. I'll be staying until the following Monday," Sin explained, and joyful relief warmed Mara's blood.

Guessing her reaction to the news, her father sent her a smiling look. "At least Sin will be here long enough to help you hang the decorations and trim the tree."

"Yes," she agreed, trying to contain some of her bubbling pleasure.

"I'm an expert at putting stars on the top of Christmas trees," Sin admitted, half in jest.

"Good, because Mara can't reach it, and I certainly can't." Her father patted the arm of his wheelchair to affirm his inability.

"Have you bought the tree?" Sin asked the question of Mara.

"Not yet." There was a breathless ring to her voice. "I was going into town today to pick one out."

"We can do it together," Sin suggested, which was just what she had wanted to do.

The day was spent purchasing the tree, carrying the boxes of decorations from the attic, setting the tree in its stand, trimming it, and arranging the Nativity scene on the mantel amid boughs of evergreens and holly. In the bottom of one of the boxes of Christmas decorations Sin found a sprig of mistletoe. Tying it with a ribbon, he hung it in the living room archway to the entry hall.

He stood beneath it, his gaze dancing in wicked invitation to Mara. Too self-conscious of her father's presence, Mara tried to ignore his message, laughing it away as a joke. Sin walked over, picked her up and ignored her embarrassed protests to stand her beneath the mistletoe, where he soundly kissed her into silence.

But it was the only kiss she received that day, a fact that gnawed at the back of her mind. The previous weekend she had had the impression that Sin was keeping her at arm's length even when he was kissing her. She had tried to ignore it by blaming it on her imagination, but the feeling of a distance between them was becoming too strong to ignore.

It returned on Sunday when she was lying beside

him on the rug in front of the fireplace at the cottage. They had gone for a walk in the snow-covered woods and had stopped at the cottage to get warm. They had all the privacy they could want, but Sin had done little more than kiss her.

The silence between them was broken only by the crackling of the flames. Mara wasn't comfortable with the silence stretching into the room. Her head was resting on a pillow from the sofa. She turned onto her side to study Sin's profile. An arm was crooked beneath his head to serve as a pillow. His eyes were closed, but she knew he wasn't sleeping.

"Did you love your wife, Sin?" she asked, tracing the woven pattern of his sweater with her fingertips. She struggled to maintain an attitude of only curious interest.

Thick male lashes lifted partially, laziness in his look. "Yes, I loved Ann. There are varying degrees of love, though, Mara. Your father loved your mother, but in a lesser degree than he loved the woman he left her for."

It wasn't a satisfactory answer, but Mara wasn't entirely certain what she had hoped to learn. She let the subject drop and rolled onto her back to stare once more at the ceiling.

"We should have brought some of your Christmas decorations from the house down here to the cottage." Sin changed the subject. "The place doesn't look very festive with Christmas just around the corner."

"We should have thought of that," she agreed, and glanced idly around the room. "I like the improvements you've made. Did you pick out the furniture or did Celene?"

"I did. Celene made a few suggestions, but the decisions and choices were mine." There was a hint of drawling amusement in his voice.

She felt slightly better about liking the place. Turning her head on the pillow, she looked at him. "Did you get bored with Celene?"

"Yes, I guess you could say that," he admitted with marked indifference for the subject.

She looked away, a frightening tightness in her throat. "Are you bored with me yet?"

Uncurling the arm from under his head, Sin used it to lever himself onto his side. He removed the pillow from beneath her head, a dark light in his gray blue eyes.

"What do you think?" he countered, an instant before his mouth covered hers.

His response told her nothing. His kiss lacked the persuasive mastery that had once fired a response from Mara. He was becoming bored with her: the knowledge burned its pain into her heart. Perhaps he wasn't already bored with her, but it was starting. Mara knew she didn't have the strength to wait until he decided to cast her aside. She wouldn't survive.

Turning away from his kiss, she twisted out of his arms and hurriedly stood up. She couldn't bear for him to go through the motions of making love to her when he felt no desire. She heard him rise and stiffened when his hands touched her shoulders.

"What's wrong?" His voice sounded puzzled.

She shrugged free of his touch. "Please don't," she asked stiffly.

"Why?" The one word carried the hint of demand.

Mara couldn't tell him the truth. There was too much chance he would argue and she would allow herself to be mistaken about her conclusion. Her only chance to stay in control of the situation was to brazen it out.

"I think the truth is that I'm becoming bored with you," she lied.

"What?" Sin caught her by the shoulders and spun her around, holding her in front of him while his gaze scanned her face.

"You said at the beginning it could possibly happen, that physical attraction waned after prolonged exposure." Mara used his theory to back up her story. "I don't feel the same thing when you hold me now as I did at first." Which was true, since her emotions had grown stronger and ran deeper.

His head was drawn back as if he didn't quite believe her. There was almost a wariness to his look. Grimness was in the thin line of his mouth.

"I know I said that," he admitted, but his tone discounted the worth of that remark in the same breath.

"I wasn't going to tell you how I felt. I know how fragile the male ego is," Mara went on, noting the way his jaw tightened at that statement. "But I decided it was better to be honest."

"What is it you're trying to say?" Sin demanded.

Staring at the front of his sweater, Mara tried not to betray how much pain it was causing to tell these lies. "I'm trying to say that there isn't any need for you to drive all this way for Christmas. There isn't anything to be gained by seeing each other anymore. If you want to come to the cottage for Christmas, that's your business. And I'm sure Adam will welcome you at the house, but...." She let the rest of the sentence trail into silence, unable to tell the ultimate lie that she wouldn't be glad to see him.

"But you wouldn't," Sin finished the sentence for her. The air of finality rang in his voice, slicing into her like a sword.

"I...I don't have any reason to be," she responded in a tightly quiet voice.

"No, I don't suppose you do." His hands fell away from her shoulders as he took a step away. "I guess there isn't any point hanging around now, either. All my things are packed. If you don't mind waiting a couple of minutes, I'll drop you off at the house on my way back to Baltimore."

Now that the moment had come, Mara would have preferred walking back to the house alone rather than riding with him. But a little voice dictated that she should accept his offer to prove that his company meant nothing to her, that she could get along without it or simply tolerate it.

"I don't mind waiting," she said. "It's cold outside."

"I'll only be a few minutes," he promised curtly, and walked toward the bedroom.

While he was gone, Mara picked up the poker and scattered the burning logs so the fire would die. But she knew it would never be that easy to put out the fire that burned for him in her heart. The full enormity of her decision was only just beginning to sink into her.

When Sin reappeared, she was able to turn and face him. Her expression was coolly composed, but she was the only one who knew how thin and brittle the ice was.

"Shall we go?" A small weekend suitcase was in his hand, and a hint of steel was in his voice. Mara walked to the door in answer.

Silence hung between them like a heavy curtain during the drive to the house. Its weight pressed on Mara until she wanted to scream away its presence.

Sin pulled into the driveway and stopped in front of the red brick house. As Mara quickly stepped out of the car, he said, "Say goodbye to Adam for me."

"I will," she agreed stiffly, and shut the door.

CHAPTER TEN

THERE WAS A LUMP as big as a Pennsylvania apple in
Mara's throat as she entered the house. The sound of
Sin's car pulling out of the driveway echoed painfully
in her ears. Her eyes smarted with large, unshed
tears.

The multicolored lights blinking on the Christmas
tree seemed garishly bright. The satin balls and silver
tinsel looked ludicrously cheerful when her heart felt
as if it were splintering in a million pieces.

The draft from the closing door sent the clump of
mistletoe swaying above her head. Mara glanced up
and an excruciating pain stabbed her breast as she remembered the way Sin had maneuvered her under it
only yesterday.

Shuddering away the memory, she grabbed the
nearest chair and pulled it under the mistletoe. Her
eyes were so blurred with tears that she could hardly
see as she stepped onto the chair seat and tugged the
ribboned mistletoe from its place.

"What are you doing, Mara?" Her father wheeled
his chair in from the study.

"I'm taking the mistletoe down. What does it
look as if I'm doing?" She spoke harshly to keep her
voice from trembling. Carefully, she avoided looking

at Adam as she pushed the chair to its former place.

"I can see you're taking down the mistletoe. What I wondered was why," he answered, patient yet curious.

"Because we don't need it hanging there. We don't need it hanging anywhere." Mara flung the mistletoe in the living room's wicker wastebasket.

"I think Sin will have a different opinion. He'll want to know what's happened to it when he comes at Christmas," Adam teased.

"He isn't coming at Christmas." A tear slipped out the corner of her eye and Mara hurriedly wiped it away before it trailed too far down her cheek.

But her furtive action was noticed by Adam. He tilted his head to one side to peer at her averted face, and a frown creased his forehead.

"What happened? Did you and Sin have an argument?" he questioned.

"Not exactly." Her voice was tight, choked by the pain clawing at her chest.

"What exactly?" He sat quietly in his wheelchair waiting for her explanation.

An inner war kept her silent for a moment. "I told him it would be best if he didn't come at Christmas," she admitted finally.

"Best for whom?" Adam lifted a dark brow in dry inquiry.

"Best for me—and for him, too, as far as that goes," Mara rushed out the answer in a burst of agitation. "It was hopeless from the beginning, if I'd known or guessed—oh, what does it matter!" She wiped angrily at another tear. "He never cared about me anyway."

"Is that what Sin told you?" her father asked after listening attentively to her declaration.

"Yes," she breathed out, her lungs hurting from the constant constriction of controlled emotion. "All he felt for me was...a sexual attraction." She chose his phrase. "Sooner or later he would have become bored and cast me aside, the same way he did Celene."

"Celene? Who's Celene?" Adam frowned.

"That redhead!" she flashed. "The one he brought along with him when he first came. Celene Taylor, with all her 'Sin, darlings.'" The cattiness of her tone didn't make her feel better.

"So you did the casting aside first?" Adam guessed.

"Yes, I had to before...." Mara swallowed the rest of the sentence. "I told him I was beginning to become bored with him, that whatever I'd felt, it was gone."

"Is it?" His gaze narrowed to pierce any shield she might try to use. "Have you stopped caring for him, Mara?"

She lifted her gaze to him, her eyes suddenly brimming over with tears she couldn't check. The anguish was written in every line of her expression for him to see. She couldn't contain her feelings or her heartbreak anymore. Gasping back a sob, she moved uncertainly toward his chair. When she reached his side, Adam took hold of one of her shaky hands, and the comfort and understanding he offered turned loose a storm of tears.

"Daddy, I love him," she sobbed, and collapsed to her knees, burying her head on his lap and hugging his lifeless legs.

One hand gripped her quaking shoulder while the other stroked her hair. "Go ahead, baby," he crooned, his own voice slightly choked with deep emotion. "Cry it all out. It's okay, honey. Believe me, it's okay."

Years of stored grief, pain and bitterness were washed away by the violent tears. Mara sobbed herself into oblivion. The soothing touch of her father's hand and the sound of his voice were her only lifeline to sanity.

Even after her mind had blanked out the pain with unconsciousness, her breath came in hiccuping sobs. Adam took off his sweater and draped it around her shoulders, letting her use his legs for a pillow. A fierce love glistened moistly in his eyes as he gazed down at her tear-streaked face.

"It's all right, daddy's here." He squeezed the words out through the lump in his throat.

It was dark when Mara finally came around. Her muscles were cramped from the unnatural position of rest, but all the pain, physical and emotional, seemed distant. A numbed haze kept it at bay.

"How do you feel?" Adam's quiet voice penetrated the protective mist.

"I...I don't know." As she rose awkwardly to her feet, the sweater slipped from around her shoulders. Mara looked at it blankly, half recognizing that it was his, but the gesture registered only dimly. She did the automatic thing and gave it back to him. "I feel...as if I've been drugged."

"Lie down on the sofa for a while," her father suggested.

Drained and without energy, Mara moved to the sofa. She murmured a halfhearted protest when Adam pulled a quilted comforter over her. She stared sightlessly at the ceiling, her mind seemingly blank.

"You lie there and rest. I'll be back in a moment," Adam promised.

Mara was barely aware of him leaving. She had no conception of how long he was gone; it could have been a minute or an hour. When he returned, he positioned his wheelchair parallel with the sofa.

"Here, take some of this." He held a spoon to her mouth. "I warmed some soup for you."

Indifferent to the appetizing aroma, her mouth remained closed until Adam forced it apart with the spoon and let the warm liquid trickle inside. She stirred under its reviving taste and was less recalcitrant at the second spoonful. Her eyes sought his in silent gratitude.

"How did you manage?" she murmured, briefly curious.

"I'm not such an invalid that I can't manage a can opener and a burner on the stove," he teased gently.

Memory flashed in Mara's mind back to a time when she had cared for her mother like this. She realized that her mother had loved none too wisely, either. Pain twisted through her.

"It hurts," she whispered.

"Yes." Adam didn't deny it. He took the apron away. "Sleep now. Life may not look so bleak in the morning."

Mara doubted it, but she obediently closed her

eyes. When she awakened the next morning, Adam was there. She felt like one big throbbing ache. But the realization that he was there, waiting on her, looking after her, made her throw aside the comforter and sit up.

"I'll make some coffee," she offered.

"Good idea." He followed he into the kitchen, not speaking again until she had plugged the coffeepot in. "Isn't there a possibility that you're mistaken about Sin?"

Hope sprang, but Mara quickly squashed it. "I only wish I were." She paused to glance at her father. "I know you like Sin, you did from the beginning, but you have to face the truth the same way I did," she said, still blessedly numbed. "I was merely attractive to him and provided him with some weekend entertainment. He probably even considered me something of a challenge." The first sting of tears since yesterday's torrent burned her eyes, and she turned away, not wanting to start weeping again. "Anyway, it's over. And I don't want to discuss it any more.

IT WAS A REFUSAL that Mara repeated twice more in the next two days whenever Adam attempted to introduce the subject. The tenuous bond between father and daughter had strengthened in the intervening time. Someday she knew she would talk to him about Sin, but not while the hurt was so fresh.

The holiday spirit was sadly lacking in their household. Staying with family tradition, they exchanged gifts on Christmas Eve. There had been two presents under the tree for Sin, one from Mara and the other from her father. Both had disappeared during the last couple of days—Adam's doing, Mara guessed, so she wouldn't be reminded that Sin had been going to celebrate Christmas with them.

Christmas morning seemed no different from recent mornings. After breakfast, Mara washed the dishes while her father retired to the living room to watch the televised Christmas services. Christmas hymns filtered joyfully into the kitchen.

An aching loneliness swept over her. Tears welled in her eyes and she began angrily slamming cupboard doors and clattering pots and pans as she put the dishes away, anything to cover the music from the living room. It didn't work very well. She finally had to stop and wipe her eyes. Sniffling a little, she put a ham roast in the oven and filled the colander with some potatoes to peel and slice for scalloped potatoes.

The singing stopped and the muffled sound of the sermon began. Mara sat in a kitchen chair at the table and began peeling the potatoes. Keeping busy, she had discovered, was therapeutic.

"Mara?" Adam called. "Come in here, will you? Santa Claus has finally delivered your present."

Glancing at the swinging door, Mara breathed out a sigh. There was a temptation to tell him she was busy, but she guessed he had manufactured some kind of surprise to boost her spirits—as if anything could.

Santa Claus. A smile tugged at her mouth. Santa Claus hadn't visited her since she was fifteen, the last

Christmas she and her parents had spent together as a family. Santa had never forgotten to leave her a present then, regardless of whether she believed in his existence or not. Perhaps her father had remembered, too.

Either way, his thoughtfulness couldn't be ignored or set aside until she was in the mood to accept it. Setting the partially peeled potato down, Mara wiped her hands on a towel.

"Coming," she answered.

As she pushed the swinging door open, she heard the front door close. *Delivered* had been the term Adam used. A curious frown drew her brows together as she wondered who would make deliveries on Christmas Day.

Her father was practically beaming when she entered the living room. His gaze swung toward the entryway and Mara's followed. She stopped short when she saw Sin framed in the opening. Dressed in a suit and tie and navy blue topcoat, he looked stern and unyielding. The hoary chill of winter seemed to sweep around him. Her heart somersaulted and leaped in unbounded joy, but fear kept her from voicing it.

"Sin!" Mara breathed his name at last. Confusion raced through her. "What are you doing here?"

His jaw hardened in savage grimness. "Adam told me you were lying. That you really want to see me."

"How...when...." She glanced at her father, her pained expression accusing him of betraying her. Was this his vengeance? To see her brought tumbling down from her pedestal?

"I telephoned him yesterday." Adam volunteered the information.

"How could you?" she demanded tightly.

"What the hell difference does it make how I found out?" Sin demanded. "All I want to know is whether he's telling me the truth. Were you lying?"

Trapped as she was, Mara was forced to admit, "Yes."

Her answer didn't seem to please him. Sin continued to glare at her across the distance of the room, intimidating her with the anger barely held in check.

"Why? Why, Mara, why?" he repeated the demand in a low growl.

"Because. . . I could tell you were getting tired of me," she replied defensively.

"I—what?!" It was an explosive reaction, disbelief and anger ringing together.

"Don't pretend you don't know what I'm talking about." Mara was stung into retorting. "You were beginning to keep a distance between us. Even when we were together, part of you seemed to remain aloof."

"From that you concluded I was getting tired of you," Sin ground out in a voice that questioned her intelligence. "It didn't ever occur to you that I'm a man with a man's appetites and that all that playing around was becoming a strain?"

Warily she drew her head back, recognizing it was possible but afraid to believe him. "No, it didn't," she admitted.

"What difference was it to you whether or not I was getting tired of you?" He changed the direction of his questions, his eyes narrowing on her. "We were just experimenting anyway, so why should you care?"

Her lips closed together mutinously, but her father supplied the answer. "She's fallen in love with you."

Sin's gaze never wavered from her face. "Is that true?" he demanded without an ounce of softness.

Angered by the attack from both sides, Mara shouted, "Yes!"

Briefly he flicked a glance to her father. "Adam, I want your permission to marry your daughter."

"Granted." Adam's dark eyes twinkled brightly at Mara's stunned expression.

Reaching into the pocket of his topcoat, Sin took something out and tossed it across the room to Mara. Sheer reflex enabled her to catch the ring box. She was dazed by the unexpected chain of events. She wasn't even certain if she knew what was happening. With shaking fingers, she opened the box. A diamond solitaire winked rainbow hues back at her.

"Will you marry me?" Sin demanded. The room still separated them.

Dragging her gaze from the ring, she looked at him. "Yes," she answered, starry-eyed and breathless.

For the first time since he had arrived, his hard features began to soften, relief mixing with another, stronger emotion. The edges of his mouth turned faintly upward.

"If you take the first step, Mara, I'll meet you halfway," Sin promised.

Mara had the giddy feeling that she floated across

her half of the room. Her feet never seemed to touch the ground. They certainly didn't when he crushed her in his arms to bruise her mouth in a possessive kiss. Her father discreetly left the room.

"I don't believe it," she gasped when he finally let her up for air. "Am I dreaming this?"

"It's no dream." His mouth moved roughly over her hair, unsatisfied not to be touching her.

"And you really love me?" She felt the shuddering force of his arms around her, but still needed the reassurance of his words.

"Yes, you crazy little fool," he muttered against her throat. "Every time I saw you I fell a little bit more in love with you until I was hopelessly lost."

"It was the same for me." Her lips began brushing feather kisses over his male features.

"After that first time I met you at the cottage, I told myself I was merely fascinated by the dark-haired, dark-eyed icicle who greeted me. It only took one brief thaw for that fascination to become something deeper." Sin stopped her teasing lips with a demanding kiss. Mara gave it back with vibrant intensity. "I should have guessed you were playing the coward again and running from me," he accused.

"I thought I was losing you," Mara tried to explain. "I decided I'd rather make the break swift and clean than let it drag on until you did it. I knew I'd be that much more in love with you and the hurt would be that much greater."

"And I was determined not to rush you into admitting an emotion when you were just learning to feel." He took some of the blame for the misunderstanding.

"What if Adam hadn't called you?" She suddenly realized she wouldn't be in Sin's arms or have his ring on her finger.

"I hadn't given up. I was just trying to come up with a new battle plan," he assured her. "Now I don't have to worry. You're going to be my wife... and soon."

"Yes," Mara agreed readily. "I would like a church wedding, though, so my... father can give me away to you."

Sin lifted his head long enough to smile at her. "I'm glad to hear you say that." Then he made sure she didn't say any more for quite a while.

"GIVE YOUR HEART TO HARLEQUIN" SWEEPSTAKES
OFFICIAL RULES
NO PURCHASE NECESSARY TO ENTER OR RECEIVE A PRIZE

1. To enter and join the Preview Service, scratch off the concealment device on all game tickets. This will reveal the values for each Sweepstakes entry number, the number of free books you will receive, and your free bonus gift as part of our Preview Service. If you do not wish to take advantage of our Preview Service, only scratch off the concealment device on game tickets 1-3. To enter, return your entire sheet of tickets.

2. Either way your Sweepstakes numbers will be compared against the list of winning numbers generated at random by computer. In the event that all prizes are not claimed, random drawings will be held from all entries received from all presentations to award all unclaimed prizes. All cash prizes are payable in U.S. funds. This is in addition to any free, surprise or mystery gifts that might be offered. Versions of this Sweepstakes with different prizes may appear in other mailings or at retail outlets by Torstar Ltd. and its affiliates. This presentation offers the following prizes:

(1)	*Grand Prize	$1,000,000 Annuity
(1)	First Prize	$25,000
(2)	Second Prize	$10,000
(5)	Third Prize	$5,000
(10)	Fourth Prize	$1,000
(2,000)	Fifth Prize	$10

. . .*This presentation contains a Grand Prize offering of a $1,000,000 annuity. Winner may elect to receive $25,000 a year for life up to $1,000,000 or $250,000 in one cash payment. Winners selected will receive the prizes offered in the Sweepstakes promotion they receive.

Entrants may cancel Preview Service at any time without cost or obligation (see details in the center insert card).

3. This promotion is being conducted under the supervision of Marden-Kane, an independent judging organization. By entering the Sweepstakes, each entrant accepts and agrees to be bound by these rules and the decisions of the judges which shall be final and binding. Odds of winning in the random drawing are dependent upon the total number of entries received. Taxes, if any, are the sole responsibility of the winners. Prizes are non-transferable. All entries must be received by March 31, 1988. The drawing will take place on April 30, 1988 at the offices of Marden-Kane, Lake Success, New York.

4. This offer is open to residents of the U.S., Great Britain and Canada, 18 years or older except employees of Torstar Ltd., its affiliates, subsidiaries, Marden-Kane and all other agencies and persons connected with conducting this Sweepstakes. All Federal, State and local laws apply. Void wherever prohibited or restricted by law.

5. Winners will be notified by mail and may be required to execute an affidavit of eligibility and release which must be returned within 14 days after notification. Canadian winners will be required to answer a skill testing question. Winners consent to the use of their name, photograph and/or likeness for advertising and publicity in conjunction with this and similar promotions without additional compensation. One prize per family or household.

6. For a list of our most current prize winners, send a stamped, self-addressed envelope to: WINNERS LIST c/o MARDEN-KANE, P.O. BOX 701, SAYREVILLE, N.J. 08872.

For the millions who can't read
Give the Gift of Literacy

One out of five adults in North America
cannot read or write well enough
to fill out a job application
or understand the directions on a bottle of medicine.

**You can change all this by joining the fight
against illiteracy.**

For more information write to:
Contact, Box 81826, Lincoln, Neb. 68501
In the United States, call toll free: 1-800-228-8813

**The only degree you need
is a degree of caring**

LIT-A-1R

Harlequin Intrigue
Adopts a New Cover Story!

**We are proud to present to you
the new Harlequin Intrigue cover design.**

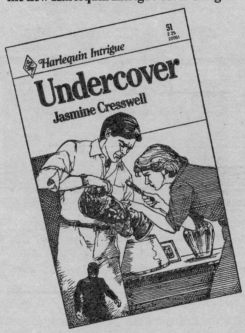

Look for two exciting new stories each month, which mix a contemporary, sophisticated romance with the surprising twists and turns of a puzzler . . . romance with "something more."

PAMELA BROWNING

...is fireworks on the green at the Fourth of July and prayers said around the Thanksgiving table. It is the dream of freedom realized in thousands of small towns across this great nation.

But mostly, the Heartland is its people. People who care about and help one another. People who cherish traditional values and give to their children the greatest gift, the gift of love.

American Romance presents HEARTLAND, an emotional trilogy about people whose memories, hopes and dreams are bound up in the acres they farm.

HEARTLAND...the story of America.

Don't miss these heartfelt stories: American Romance #237 SIMPLE GIFTS (March), #241 FLY AWAY (April), and #245 HARVEST HOME (May).

HRT-1

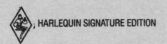 HARLEQUIN SIGNATURE EDITION

CAROLE MORTIMER

JUST ONE NIGHT

Hawk Sinclair—Texas millionaire and owner of the exclusive
Sinclair hotels, determined to protect his son's inheritance.
Leonie Spencer—desperate to protect her sister's happiness.

They were together for just one night.
The night their daughter was conceived.

Blackmail, kidnapping and attempted murder add suspense
to passion in this exciting bestseller.

The success story of Carole Mortimer continues with *Just
One Night*, a captivating romance from the author of the
bestselling novels, *Gypsy* and *Merlyn's Magic*.

**Available in March
wherever paperbacks are sold.**

WTCH-1